SAVING SERENA

SAVING SERENA

An Undersea Tale of Love, Treachery, and Betrayal

A novella

BEVERLEY SCHERBERGER

Copyright © 2016 by Beverley Scherberger

ISBN -13: 978-1541276413
ISBN- 10: 1541276418

Createspace Independent Publishing Platform
North Charleston, South Carolina

This is a work of fiction. Names, characters, and incidents are a product of the author's imagination. Locales and public names are sometimes used for atmospheric purposes. Any resemblance to actual people, living or dead, or to businesses, companies, or events is entirely coincidental.

Printed in the United States of America

ACKNOWLEDGMENTS

FIRST AND FOREMOST, I want to say a warm "Thank you!" to friends and family, co-workers, and Cotacachi Writers Club members — all have been instrumental in encouraging me and, occasionally, delivering a kick-start to the seat of my pants. For this I am sincerely grateful.

Nearly 30 years ago, a former co-worker read the short story that eventually developed into this novella. Her profound, gut-wrenching reaction made such an impression I knew that someday I would have to expound upon those original ten pages. Thank you, Diane, for the tears you shed.

And last but not least, I'd like to acknowledge the entire team who made telling this story possible. My friend Ted Jones designed the cover and the folks at Createspace fielded my many questions.

Once published, though, *you* – the readers – are the most important component of its success. So here's a heartfelt "THANK YOU!" to everyone who leapt off the boat and swam with the mermaids. May *you* always have a second chance at your dreams, too.

OTHER TITLES BY BEVERLEY SCHERBERGER

CHAPTER 1

THE CALM, SUN-DAPPLED WATER surrounding the dive boat suddenly erupted with playful dolphins. The bright, late morning sunlight glinted off their wet bodies and all twelve divers squealed with excited anticipation. Each of us had longed for an opportunity to swim with the intelligent, curious animals, so when the easy-going captain threw up his hands, chuckled at our reaction, and laughingly hollered, "Okay! Go!" we grabbed our fins and leapt back into the water.

The sea closed over my head as I scanned the blue for their sleek, graceful forms, their sonar clicks and whistles seeming to come from all directions. Immediately, though, I knew something was wrong. Kicking fairly hard, I still descended much more rapidly than I should have. I groaned.

As the last diver to climb aboard the boat following our fifty-minute dive this morning, I hadn't shed all of my gear before the dolphins appeared. In my excitement, I had jumped off the boat still wearing mask, snorkel, and fins—and a ten pound weight belt.

Reluctant to send over a hundred dollars-worth of gear to the bottom of the ocean without trying to resolve the problem, I kicked harder, hoping I could reach the boat and grab the lowest ladder rung without releasing the belt. I gulped air and then sank below the surface, kicking madly toward the boat. Frantic kicks sent me back to the surface where I grabbed a quick breath and sank again. I repeated the process over and over and made slow but steady progress.

I was tiring. The combined effort of holding my breath and kicking forcefully enough to move upward and closer to the boat were taking their toll. I determined to make one last-ditch effort to reach the ladder. Then it was adios to the weight belt.

Okay, I was nearly there. I could see the ladder only a few feet ahead and above me. One powerful kick should get me close enough to grab the bottom rung.

As I lunged upward, one arm raised over my head to reach for the ladder, the boat rose lazily on a large swell and dropped heavily into the trough. Unfortunately, my lunge had positioned me directly below the corner of the stern. The metal rung hit my raised arm sharply, snapping the bone cleanly just below the elbow; the boat's impact with my skull drove my body deep below the surface.

Sometime later, my eyes sprang open to see endless deep blue water…above, below, and all around. I clawed and kicked and struggled, trying desperately to make my way to the hopelessly distant surface. As my heart beat a wild rhythm and adrenaline surged through my veins, my uncooperative right arm sent piercing daggers of pain up my shoulder.

I spotted sudden movement to the left and whirled to face it. What type of undersea creature might be approaching? A large turtle? An enormous fish? Or something more menacing? My heart continued its wild tempo as my eyes strained to put a definitive shape to the shadow in the distance, my lungs now screaming for air.

Immobile, exerting as little energy as possible while the form drew near, I was both fascinated and mystified as it assumed a definite female shape. It looked like... It couldn't be... They didn't *really exist*, did they? I wracked my brain in an attempt to recall if I'd ever heard of a documented instance of an encounter with a mermaid. Unless I was hallucinating, I was face-to-face with one of these mythical beings: a mermaid with the face and curvaceous torso of a lovely young woman and the muscular tail of a fish. UN-believable!

Reminiscent of Lady Godiva, her mass of long blonde curls drifted lazily around her body, first hiding, then exposing creamy white skin and full, firm breasts. Her narrow waist flared out at the hips where the skin blended seamlessly into blue-grey, overlapping scales that shimmered in the water. They reflected and magnified the muted ambient light like thousands of tiny mirrors.

Slowly, she swam closer. Mesmerized, I studied every detail of this amazingly graceful creature: high cheekbones, a patrician nose, full lips, and wide blue eyes. Her powerful tail slowly curved, unfurled, and curved again, providing stability and maintaining a vertical position in the water. Radiating curiosity, concern, and uncertainty, her face also expressed warmth and kindness.

Cocking her head slightly to the right, she examined me just as intensely as I scrutinized her. She seemed to understand my dire situation and smiled reassuringly.

Cautiously, I smiled back, almost against my will—and in total disbelief. Miraculously, my lungs no longer strained for air and my body relaxed. Breathing normally, I let out a sigh of relief even though I didn't understand a thing that was happening.

Encouraged by my smile, she floated up and extended her hand. Tentatively, I reached out to gingerly touch her fingers, nearly afraid I grasped for a mirage. At my touch, her smile widened, showing perfect white teeth and her strong fingers clasped mine in friendship. I flinched, shocked to find a tangible hand holding mine.

When her eyes darted past me, I let go and twisted fearfully in the water to see what was approaching from behind. Astonished, I discovered another mermaid stopping some distance away, her wavy black hair floating like long spider webs in the water. Light, café au lait skin, small, perky breasts, and a slim, almost boyish physique suggested a much younger age. The scales of her tail glistened a brilliant green at the hips then blended into a burnished copper at the bottom. Shy and seemingly afraid to draw near, she held back, her dark eyes wide with fascination and trepidation—this creature looked like her, yet did not. She hovered about a dozen feet away, gaping at my mask and snorkel and the neon pink Lycra wetskin encasing me from neck to ankle. The fact that I sported two legs instead of a fish-tail seemed cause for concern.

The blonde mermaid coaxed the brunette into swimming closer and motioned for her to take my other hand. I pointed to my broken right arm and vigorously shook my head, "No!" They understood my injury and the brunette darted off, purpose apparent in every flick of her tail.

When she reappeared a short time later with a ten-inch branch of coral and a length of kelp, she overcame her initial fear and helped the blonde splint my arm, using the strong fibers to secure it. Although they handled the limb carefully, I nearly blacked out from the excruciating pain. When my vision cleared, I could see empathy in their eyes. The blonde then floated in front of me and cautiously backed into my front. The brunette helped me wrap my good arm around the blonde's waist, gently sandwiching the broken limb between our bodies.

Using the remaining long piece of kelp, the brunette lashed us together. Once satisfied I was secure, the blonde swam slowly, jostling my arm as little as possible, and I appreciated her consideration.

Amazed at the power in the mermaid's tail at this slow pace, I could imagine being propelled through the water at astonishing speeds. I wondered at our destination since this had been a most amazing day and I suspected the surprises weren't over yet.

CHAPTER 2

WE SAILED OVER sandy bottom, stands of spiky Elkhorn coral, and deep blue water, finally cruising to a halt at the edge of a coral reef. The brunette untied me and I watched the girls glide gracefully down the side of the drop-off to a nearly invisible opening hidden amidst some large boulders and lacy sea fans. Unwilling to be left behind, I followed and saw the young brunette disappear into the fissure. The blonde moved aside, smiled reassuringly, and motioned for me to enter.

Slightly apprehensive, I gently fluttered my fins and floated in through the opening. Narrow at first, the entrance widened as it curved slightly to the right. Once around the corner, the floor dropped away, the ceiling soared high above, and the unbelievable scene took my breath away. We hovered above an enormous cavern inhabited by many mermaids, mermen, and merkids going about apparently normal daily lives. But then, what was *normal* about any of this? I shook my head in an effort to dispel the hallucination but when I looked again, the image remained.

From this vantage point, I observed many couples and families; mermaids and mermen as different from one another as regular people, but all with those incredible, scaly-yet-beautiful, iridescent fish-tails. I noted that the tails came in a variety of colors: silver, gold, copper, green, blue, pink, and nearly everything in between. The mermaids looked strong and muscular while the mermen seemed slimmer and less physically imposing.

I tore my gaze away from the mesmerizing scene when the blonde motioned for me to follow her. I spotted the young brunette peeking around a nearby stone wall. She smiled shyly as we passed and ducked quickly out of sight. The blonde and I cruised along the wall to the floor of the cavern where an older couple relaxed while others served snacks.

As we neared the couple, I noticed a less casual demeanor in those speaking or interacting with this regal, more elderly pair. Heads bowed slightly when approaching or taking leave. No merkids scampered about. Individuals waited on them with obvious respect and reverence. I suspected this couple was held in high regard and possibly even ruled this underwater society.

The blonde stopped about fifteen feet in front of the pair and bowed her head dutifully. I followed suit, figuring it wouldn't do to offend the leaders when I so desperately needed their help. The elderly woman greeted my companion with a smile and apparent affection and I realized I could clearly understand them.

"Maia, who do you bring before us? She is quite visibly not one of our own."

Maia graciously introduced me. "Tinami and Saya, leaders of our sirene, I bring a lost one before you today, injured and in need of help. She is no threat to our people and comes as a friend. I ask for your compassion and wisdom in this matter. I hope to offer this lost one medical attention, food, and temporary lodging."

At their urging, Maia gave a detailed description of how she had found me drifting, injured and panicky.

Saya then addressed me. "Lost one, what name are you known by?"

As I opened my mouth to reply, this most familiar bit of information eluded me and I realized I couldn't recall my name.

Panic and confusion must have shown plainly on my face since Saya kindly intervened. "Don't worry. Often, a blow to the head causes memory lapse and the lump on your forehead indicates that may be the source of your forgetfulness. For now, we'll call you Serena."

Raising my hand to my throbbing head, I smiled gratefully and nodded my thanks as she continued her gentle questions.

"How is it you came to these depths? Humans rarely venture this deep."

I related as many details as I could recall, confirming her suspicion of a blow to the head. Suddenly, I wanted nothing more than a place to lie down, feeling a bit woozy.

Tinami and Saya discussed the situation in low voices.

I caught only a couple phrases: "injuries healed" and "return to the surface." As I awaited their decision, I felt weak from hunger and the stress of the day, my head and arm both throbbed horribly, and I had no idea how I could possibly return to My Life Before Today.

Finally, the royal couple addressed us. "Maia, take Serena to the vacant cubicle we use for occasional guests. She can stay until her injuries heal."

Saya then turned to me. "Serena, our doctor will see you immediately and a meal will be delivered to your room shortly. If there's anything you need, please ask. We don't have many guests and would like to take this opportunity to offer our complete hospitality." She directed one of the servants to fetch the doctor. Relieved, I smiled and bowed my head.

As Tinami and Saya turned to each other and began discussing a different topic, Maia and I slipped away. We swam past numerous family homes to an empty cubicle with an interesting-looking bed and small side table made of rock. She pointed and smiled kindly.

"Lie down and get some rest. The doctor will be here soon." She swam off, leaving me to take her advice.

I eyed the unusual bed and approached it for closer inspection. Comprised of half of a large clam shell, it contained several layers of sea fans atop a deep bed of soft sand. In spite of my situation, it looked inviting.

Lying down slightly eased the throbbing pain and that's where Maia found me a short while later. She gently woke me to introduce a thin, elderly mermaid with a kind smile named Kalani who'd come to address my broken arm while the doctor dealt with a sick child.

First, Kalani pressed her hand to my forehead like Mom used to do. Satisfied my temperature was normal, she then skillfully pried open an oyster shell and scooped the small, still-wriggling creature out into my hand. At my look of disgust, she smiled sympathetically. "It will help ease the pain as I set your broken arm. It'll also soothe your stomach and help you sleep. Please, chew it thoroughly and swallow quickly."

I had no reason not to trust her, so fighting revulsion I popped the little creature into my mouth. Chomping and gnawing on the stringy meat, I nearly gagged at its texture and bitter taste. Thankfully, saliva filled my mouth and helped wash the nasty bitterness off my tongue.

Kalani tenderly examined the contusion on my forehead. "You'll soon have a really ugly bruise here. The doctor should look at it tomorrow. If you develop a stabbing headache, severe dizziness, or impaired vision tonight, please send someone to fetch either the doctor or myself. Would you like someone to sit with you for a while?"

"I'll be fine. In fact, I'm feeling drowsy now. After the kind of day I've had, I doubt I'll have any trouble sleeping."

Convinced the medicinal oyster had taken effect, she deftly set my broken arm with a minimum of fuss or additional pain, finally wrapping it neatly with kelp. Once sure it was exactly right, she smeared a thick, dark, tarry substance over it and said, "This will harden in about fifteen minutes. You need to stay as still as possible until then." She kindly patted my shoulder, a gentle smile crinkling her eyes at the corners, and left Maia and me alone.

Maia stayed until the cast had hardened. A servant delivered a dinner tray as she was preparing to leave and I groaned inwardly at her parting words, wondering what the meal would consist of. "Please eat your dinner. It will help you regain your strength." She left and I turned to examine the repast before me.

In spite of a faint, lingering nausea, I gingerly tasted each item, surprised to find everything very flavorful. I savored the taste of lobster with a side salad of, could it be, kelp? I had no idea what spices they used down here on the ocean floor, but my tongue recognized the familiar tang of salt and pepper, as well as a delicate hint of rosemary and lemon. A small rounded shell containing something resembling a fruit cobbler tempted me to try dessert. A cobbler? Here? I tentatively took a small spoonful and the sweet flavor of unusual berries flooded my mouth. I gobbled the entire bowl, mentally thanking whatever mer-chef had prepared this delectable concoction.

I managed to down every morsel, although eating with my left hand forced me to eat slowly. With a full stomach and Kalani's sleep aid, I immediately dozed off on my sea-fan-and-sand bed and didn't wake until morning.

The lump on my head ached and I assumed I had a huge ugly bruise that would remain for quite a while, however, I suffered no further nausea. My arm still throbbed within the awkward cast, but the initial sharp pain of the break had lessened. In spite of the discomfort, I felt energized, couldn't wait to explore my surroundings and meet some of my neighbors, and hoped Maia would soon appear to show me around.

I impatiently peeked past the rough stone wall of my cubicle and surveyed a hustle-bustle of activity. It took a moment to realize I didn't see any mermaids, only mermen and merkids. As I pondered where the females might be, the young brunette who had helped Maia rescue me the day before appeared at my side, startling me out of my reverie.

"Good morning, Serena. My name is Kiki." She carried breakfast on a thin slice of rectangular stone and placed it on the bedside table. Ducking her head shyly, she said softly, "If you feel up to it, after breakfast I can give you a tour." She blushed and smiled at my eager response.

"Oh, yes, I'd like that!"

Kiki returned shortly after I finished eating the unusual granola ground and shaped into a bar. It seemed like a mixture of grains and nuts with some fruity berries thrown in—similar to the fruit in last night's cobbler.

She waited while I clumsily donned my fins. I wasn't accustomed to putting them on with only one hand, but knew I couldn't swim fast enough without them to keep up with her. We meandered through the enormous cavern, stopping often to chat with inquisitive neighbors. The merkids, especially, were enthralled by my legs and often swam up behind me to touch them with feather-light fingers. When I turned to smile at them, they giggled and darted quickly away, peering out curiously from behind the rock walls.

Recalling Kiki's shyness, I encouraged her to talk about her people. "Why is a group of mer-people called a 'sirene'?"

Blushing again, she related a fascinating tale. "Long ago, unlike today, there were no taboos about mer-people going to the surface. Our ancestors used to play in the surf and enjoy the warmth of the sun." She hung her head and paused for a moment before continuing. "Our lore tells of a group of beautiful young mermaids who lured a ship onto the rocks so they could play with the men, many of whom perished when the ship sank. Frightened and horrified at what they'd done, the mermaids swam into deep water and the remaining humans drowned. Since then, our kind have been called sirens and the name sirene has been adopted to indicate a group of mer-people—like a school of fish or a pod of dolphins."

I frowned, contemplating the tale, and asked another question. "Why am I able to breathe so comfortably?"

"I have heard stories of a few humans who have survived with us as long as they are in close proximity to mer-people. It used to happen more frequently when we were allowed to visit the surface, but from what I understand, it's been over one hundred years since humans have lived with us.

"Maia and I had pushed the limits of where we're allowed to go and were enjoying the warmer water where we found you. And since you are now surrounded by our kind, you are in no danger of drowning."

That explanation made as much sense as anything else I'd experienced recently so I turned my attention to the cavern and its inhabitants. Curious about not seeing any females, I asked, "Where are all the mermaids? I only see mermen and merkids."

As Kiki explained, I enjoyed the musical lilt in her voice. "Mer-people are like the seahorse people. The males have babies and raise the children. The mermaids take care of everyone by going out every morning to hunt for food."

Smiling broadly, she puffed out her pre-adolescent chest and boasted, "Next year, I'll be old enough to hunt with the women." Then she slouched and groused, "But until then, I have to stay with the men and the children. I'm old enough, really I am! What difference does one year make?" Her lower lip pushed out in a pout she murmured, "I feel like a glorified babysitter."

I remembered feeling too old to be a child and too young to be a woman and wanted to help Kiki believe she was doing something important. I peppered her with questions about life in the sirene and she was soon chattering happily in reply. We swam and talked as I absorbed information about this fascinating new world.

Completely engrossed in Kiki's answer to another of my many questions, I abruptly collided with someone exiting the common area. He had been looking the other way and his sharply exhaled "Oomph!" indicated I had hit pretty hard.

I yelped in pain at the impact and he quickly turned to face me. I completely forgot both the pain and the apology that was on my lips. Gazing into the greenest eyes I'd ever seen, I stammered, "Uh, um... Sorry... Wasn't looking... where..." My voice trailed off as my mind went blank.

Long dark lashes framed magnificent green eyes, silver hair with just a hint of curl brushed the back of his neck, and a strong, square jaw hinted at strength and determination. Drawn back to those eyes, I realized he was easily the best-looking man

13

I'd ever seen. And that deep cleft in his chin had me longing to trace it with my tongue.

His murmured, "Excuse me" jolted me back to my senses.

"I'm *so* sorry. I was caught up in what Kiki was saying. Are you alright?"

His dazzling smile showed off full lips and even white teeth, the sexy combination threatening to send me on another mental journey elsewhere. Kiki rescued me again and introduced us. His name was Nathan and he chuckled softly and murmured, "What a beautiful name" when she told him I was called Serena.

With a twinkle in his eyes, he assured me he had survived our collision and then commented on the ugly bruise and the cast on my arm. "Are you in the habit of running into things?" he asked jokingly.

Flustered, I didn't want to launch into an implausible-sounding story so was greatly relieved when Nathan excused himself to go check on a child that began to cry nearby. As he swam away, I couldn't help but notice his muscular physique and the bronze-colored scales that deepened to a glittering black at the tail fin.

Young enough to be oblivious to the effect Nathan had had on me, Kiki launched into a sad story, complete with as many details as she could recall. I listened intently.

"Nathan was older than most mermen when he got married because he studied for a long time with the sirene's doctor. He needed to learn as much as he could before the old merman died. It's really important for every sirene to have its own doctor since we live far enough apart to not overlap when hunting. Finally, Tinami and Saya told Nathan he had to get married. I don't know why."

Kiki shrugged her shoulders and rattled on with her story, not realizing I hung on every detail. "They were only married a little while when Nathan's wife was killed in a hunting accident. It was a shark. And I guess our laws say he has to wait for two years before getting married again. But he doesn't seem to mind. I never see him with any of the mermaids, anyway. And he keeps busy helping with the merkids and taking care of anybody who gets sick. He's lucky since we're pretty healthy."

I tuned out some of her ramblings. *Hmm... That means those green eyes aren't spoken for.*

My head and arm had begun to throb in earnest and after the collision with Nathan I had to constantly drag my errant thoughts back to Kiki's monologue. Since I could no longer concentrate on her tour, I suggested she lead me back to my cubicle. There, I stretched out on the bed where visions of green eyes and silver hair brought a faint smile to my lips. I fell into a deep and restful sleep.

CHAPTER 3

WHEN THE MERMAIDS returned from hunting later that afternoon, Maia came to visit and brought Dr. Nathan to examine me. When they entered my cubicle, I nearly fell off the bed in surprise. "Oh, I didn't realize.... You're the doc...?"

As I clumsily scrambled off the bed, I stubbed my toe on the side table and nearly tripped, stumbling right into his arms. He righted me and I stammered, "Sorry. I'm not usually... Um..."

I could see he found the incident tremendously amusing by the twinkle in those green eyes and the soft smile that curled the corners of his lips.

Maia seemed puzzled by my behavior and gave me a questioning look, but when Dr. Nathan suggested he check my injuries, she discreetly swam off to give us some privacy.

He closely observed my movements as I swallowed another of the repulsive medicinal oysters and explained that "...such a severe blow to the head could cause serious delayed reactions involving motor skills and slurred speech." His tone turned light and mischievous as he added, "I want to be sure your motor skills are normal and, if you could actually speak an entire sentence, I'll know whether your speech has been affected."

His taunt produced the desired result. "How *dare* you come in here and accuse me of being some kind of half-wit that can't utter a complete sentence! My speech is just fine, thank you, and if you'll finish your examination, I'll just..." I stopped in mid-sentence when he laughed aloud at my outburst. I then detected his rakishly raised eyebrow and the twinkle in his eyes.

With arms crossed over his chest, he goaded me once more. "Go on, Serena, my exam won't be complete unless you throw something at me so I can check your motor skills!"

As I grabbed a conch shell decorating the side table, Dr. Nathan whirled and streaked for the door.

When he peeked around the door opening, I glared at him in mock fury until he relented.

"Okay, okay, I'm only teasing. Can't you two-tailed people take a joke?"

I threatened to throw the conch shell again and we both burst into laughter.

"Now, can I come back in and check that bump on your head?"

"Yes, as long as you reign in that sarcastic sense of humor."

Dr. Nathan swam back into the room and stopped close in front of me. As his fingers probed the still-painful contusion on my head, I could feel the heat from his body. I blushed at his touch.

"You're warm and slightly flushed. Do you feel feverish?"

"I'm fine." I quickly changed the subject. "Do you think I could swim outside the cavern tomorrow?"

With that sparkle back in his eyes but a serious look on his face, he nodded thoughtfully. "I think physical therapy might be beneficial. I could give you a tour to gauge how you handle it and to be sure you don't overexert yourself. I don't want you reinjuring that arm. And it'll give me the chance to monitor that spectacular bruise you're sporting, too. I'll meet you here at 10:00 tomorrow morning." He was smiling as he swam off; I was smiling as Maia returned.

"He thinks I should have physical therapy."

"Sounds like a great idea!" Maia left me to rest as the medicinal oyster forced my eyes closed once again.

After dinner that night, I felt restless and visited the common room to watch the merkids who reminded me of a throng of tadpoles darting about in a small pool. They were adorable and loved to play with my short blonde hair and strange legs, calling me Two-Tails when they thought I couldn't hear. That frenetic energy soon wore me out and I retired early, anxious for morning to come so I could swim outside with Nathan. Weird dreams of boats, drifting alone in deep blue water, and exotic green-eyed dolphins plagued my sleep.

However, I awoke refreshed and famished, thankful that Tinami and Saya's wait staff delivered breakfast to my room early. I devoured it hungrily, no longer afraid of what strange food might show up on my plate, and then watched the clock as the minutes crept by.

Finally, I heard someone at the door and leapt up excitedly to grab my fins. Kiki had come by to ask if I wanted to go for a swim. A plausible excuse escaped me, but just then Nathan appeared.

"Are you ready?"

"Oh," Kiki exclaimed, "you already have a swim partner. Have fun!" I could swear there was something in her voice that told me she suddenly understood my stammering reaction to crashing into Nathan the day before. Her giggle drifted back to us on a rippling wave as she disappeared around the corner.

"Are you sure you're up to a swim?" Nathan visually checked me over before allowing me to don my fins.

18

"I'm fine," I assured him as he eyed my impressive bruise.

We swam slowly to the cavern entrance where he said, "Stay here for a moment. I want to be sure nothing dangerous is lurking outside."

Impressed at his gallantry, I smiled to myself. *Hm... Chivalry is surely not dead here in this undersea world.*

He motioned for me to join him and we cruised slowly along the wall of the coral reef, enjoying the colorful fish, the various sponges, and the soft corals and sea fans swaying in the gentle current. I saw bright cobalt tangs; brilliant Queen and Emperor angelfish; yellowtail snappers; and even spotted a lean, green moray eel peeking from under a coral overhang. Huge schools of small silvery fish turned and circled as one, choreographed to a tune we couldn't hear. A monstrous barracuda, easily six feet long, glided slowly by, eyeing the tiny silver fish. With his mouthful of razor-sharp teeth, he could catch his fill in no time and I was glad we weren't on the menu.

We rounded a corner of the reef and the sea floor rose up in a sandy swell. In shallower water, the white bottom sported crabs, shrimp, and garden eels poking their heads up out of the sand like foot-long, petal-less flowers. As we neared, the slim eels retreated back into their holes, the sand looking barren without them.

Various types of starfish provided bright spots of color against the light background: skinny, five-legged bright blue ones, a pillow-y, six-legged red one, and an enormous tan starfish that brightened to orange at the ends of its legs all caught my eye.

Before long, the bottom dropped off and in the distance, the water darkened to a blue sapphire. I detected movement in the depths and wondered if a shark was swimming just out of sight.

As we glided alongside the vertical wall, I delighted in the swaying soft corals and sea fans. They looked fine and delicate, like Grandma's lace tablecloths. Peering closely, Nathan and I spotted numerous tiny shrimp and fish peeking out of their holes in the coral wall, eyes and antennae warily following our progress.

An avid diver, I had never enjoyed the underwater world as much as I did that day. With the water warm and clear and the visibility limitless, I reveled in the freedom of swimming without bulky scuba gear. Until now, I'd never realized how constricting and cumbersome the equipment was—I felt free as the fish around me.

Nathan and I spoke little, appreciating each other's company and synchronizing our kicks so we swam at the same speed. I felt like I could go on forever, as long as I didn't swim alone.

Finally, he stopped. "We should go back. It's not safe to swim too far from home."

Recalling Kiki's story of his wife's death, I understood and respected his caution. Keeping the wall to our left, we followed it back the way we'd come and were nearly to the entrance when Nathan pointed out a small octopus that blended almost perfectly into the background. As it flowed and undulated over the bottom, twisting and turning effortlessly through the brightly colored, sharp-edged coral and convoluted sponges, I saw it change colors to match the differing shades: brown to tan to red to blue and back to brown again. The chameleon-like performance held our rapt attention. Finally, the octopus stopped at a small opening and reached inside with one of its legs. Moments later, it flowed away from the hole with a small crab held firmly in its grasp. The serenity of the day turned a bit more somber as the crab struggled futilely for survival. The octopus easily won the mismatched contest and gobbled its lunch.

Until that moment, I hadn't considered the life and death battles that ensured survival of only the strongest and fittest. I suddenly understood how remarkably lucky I was that Maia and Kiki had found me when they did.

Nathan accompanied me to my cubicle door. "If you'd like, we could make this a daily therapy session, barring any medical emergencies, of course. It would give me a chance to keep an eye on that bruise and the broken arm."

"Yes, I'd enjoy that! I'll see you in the morning." As he swam away I was already looking forward to tomorrow.

Kiki would occasionally stop by to say hello but she never again came to my cubicle at 10 a.m. Nathan and I often waved to her as we swam to or from the entrance on our daily excursions. From her smile and friendly wave, I think she secretly approved of our budding relationship, whatever that might be.

We often followed the same route for several days and then Nathan would switch things up and we'd head in the opposite direction. I think he wanted me to never get bored and would point out various items of interest.

One day we spotted a snake slithering along the sea floor, flicking its tongue in and out like the snakes I'd seen on the Discovery Channel. Large gold spots adorned its three-foot-long, cream-colored body and I stopped, thinking it might be deadly.

Seeing my reaction, Nathan said, "That's a Gold-Spotted Eel, not a snake, and it's totally harmless—unless you're a small fish, that is." He smiled and I relaxed, knowing I was in good hands.

I got a kick out of the Hermit Crab that would find a shell abandoned by some other creature, clean it out, and make it his new home. Many months later, when he'd out-grown this shell, he would find another, larger shell and begin the process anew. If I looked closely, I could see his eyes protruding from the shell opening, intent on not becoming dinner for something larger than himself.

Nathan once pointed out a tiny little orange seahorse hiding in a stand of soft coral. It looked fragile, its prehensile tail holding it firmly in place. With no means of defense other than its bony body, I knew the tiny creature could change color to blend with its surroundings, becoming nearly invisible to predators hunting for a tasty morsel.

I recalled what Kiki had said about the mermen resembling the seahorse in giving birth and rearing the young. I had many questions but didn't feel comfortable broaching that subject with Nathan—it seemed so personal. Another day, perhaps.

Later, he showed me how to spot a cleaning station where small fish or shrimp clean the gills, scales, and teeth of larger fish. With my new skills, I spied a little red and white striped shrimp with long white antennae sitting on a rock, vigorously waggling his antennae, up and down, up and down. A large, fat sea bass stopped in front of the shrimp and opened his mouth, remaining totally motionless. Amazed, I watched the shrimp hop into the fish's mouth, thoroughly clean his teeth, and then crawl out through the gills, scouring as he went.

Nathan told me the waggling antennae indicated the shrimp was "open for business" so fish in need of a cleaning could stop on in. With the mutually beneficial relationship, the shrimp knew he was safe and would not be eaten. The fish needed the cleaners or they would suffer from parasites and diseases; the shrimp depended on the fish for food.

One morning, after we'd been swimming together every day for several weeks, Nathan grabbed my hand and slowed to a stop, pointing out a black-tipped reef shark cruising along the edge of a coral wall. His demeanor hardened as he explained. "When a shark is meandering slowly along the reef, relaxed and minding its own business, you have nothing to fear—it's simply patrolling its territory. But if it's feeling agitated, threatened, or is focused on prey, the shark will hunch his back, forcing his pectoral fins into a downward position, and swim erratically with sharp movements and quick, tight turns. That would be a good time to give the shark a wide berth and swim in the opposite direction."

When he finished talking, we watched the shark for a few more minutes and Nathan maintained his hold on my hand. Afterwards, we swam along, hand-in-hand, for quite a while. I felt comfortable and safe with him. I wondered if seeing the shark reminded him of his wife's death and decided to broach the subject. If he wanted to tell me about it, I was willing to listen. If he didn't, I wouldn't push.

"Nathan, I've heard bits and pieces of what happened to your wife. I'd like to hear it from you, if you wouldn't mind talking about it." I held my breath, hoping I hadn't overstepped.

At first, I wasn't sure he was going to respond. Then he stopped and turned to face me, still holding my hand. He looked into my eyes as he began to speak, his voice soft and low. "I was born into a different sirene, not Tinami and Saya's, and lived with my parents and four siblings until I was ten. I'd always had unusual interests for a young merkid and didn't fit in well with the rest of my age group. They wanted to play and chase and hunt while I wanted to know why and how illness and disease could be cured, how broken limbs could mend. Hanging out with the doctor was more exciting to me than playing games."

I could picture Nathan as a little merkid, pestering with curious questions.

He smiled faintly at the memory, looked away, and then continued, his voice becoming more somber. "Our sirene developed a debilitating illness and one by one, I watched friends and family waste away and die. The doctor was helpless in the face of the disease and, in fact, succumbed to it himself. My entire family died. When there were only five of us left, we set out to find another sirene that might be willing to take us in. It was risky since some groups were known for killing anyone they encountered, considering them competition for food. Others looked more kindly upon those less fortunate."

His eyes took on a sad, far-away look as he recalled the pain of losing his family and the hunger and desperation of those few remaining. After a brief pause, he resumed his story.

"We swam for many days before meeting a hunting party. They took pity on the hungry, bedraggled, and exhausted group and led us here. Luckily, we'd found Tinami and Saya's sirene.

"I was the only merkid in our group and without parents to look after me I didn't know what would become of me. But Tinami and Saya opened their hearts to me, took me in as one of their own, and treated me like a son. Unlike most mermen marriages, they had a deep love for each other that spilled over into the treatment of their people. I promised myself I would one day repay them by becoming the sirene doctor. And I longed for a marriage like theirs, not an arranged merger meant only to foster the health and prosperity of the group."

His eyes lost the sadness as he remembered growing up in a loving family home. That love had helped shape him into the caring merman he was today. I felt grateful to Tanami and Saya for their part in his development and for allowing me to stay in the sirene after my accident. I was even more grateful to have met this amazing merman, to have him in my life.

"In true merman tradition, I was promised to Saralee in an arranged marriage by the time I was twelve, but since I was studying to become a doctor, I was not forced to marry by the age of sixteen.

"Saralee was a beautiful mermaid, kind and gentle, but I had watched Tinami and Saya and yearned for more than a marriage of convenience. In some arranged marriages, the couples develop feelings for each other and become true lovers, but most are simply business arrangements. A few are disastrous."

His voice took on a tenderness I hadn't heard before and he looked deep into my eyes. I felt he was speaking to me with more than just words and my heart yearned to respond.

"I wanted more—I wanted passion and love that would sustain us until we were old and grey. I wanted to laugh and share my innermost secrets with a soul mate that understood me like no other. Although Saralee was a good mermaid and would have made a wonderful provider for our family, I felt only fondness for her. So I made excuses not to marry. I studied and kept busy with my work for as long as I could, hoping a solution would present itself." He let out a deep breath, resignation plain on his face.

"Finally, Tinami and Saya ran out of patience and insisted that Saralee and I marry. They had done so much for me that I couldn't refuse."

Nathan paused and when he continued the story, emotion roughened his voice. "Two months into our marriage, Saralee left on a hunting trip early one morning and didn't return. A shark attacked her... She was so young..." His voice broke as he confessed, "I didn't love her and I feel so guilty for trying to pretend I was happy…"

I wanted to hold him, to console him, to tell him it would be alright, but how could I? *Would* it be alright?

Squeezing his hand, I offered a reassuring smile. "Thank you for telling me, Nathan. It's natural to feel badly about Saralee's death. But feeling guilty isn't going to help. You have to get on with your life and look for that love and passion you so desire. If Saralee was the caring woman you say she was, she wouldn't have wanted your life to end just because hers did." I stopped there, afraid of saying too much, and motioned for us to continue our swim.

That day, I felt very close to Nathan and was reluctant to see him go. Later, as I attempted to relax in my cubicle, I had a mental conversation with myself regarding my feelings. *What are you doing? What if he doesn't feel the same way you do? It's hard enough to fall in love with a _human_ man—how do you expect a relationship with a merman to work?* I had many questions and very few answers.

CHAPTER 4

WITH TIME ON MY HANDS, I'd begun spending the late afternoon hours with Kalani, learning about her research and "old ways" of healing. A warm, intelligent mermaid, she cared deeply about the well-being of the sirene. In years past, each sirene had retained a medicine man or woman, but as the field of medicine grew and changed, educated doctors were in great demand. Eventually, Tinami and Saya recruited a physician to replace Kalani and she began doing research in her lab, only occasionally treating illnesses or injuries, helping the doctor on an as-needed basis.

A very hands-on type of teacher, Kalani encouraged me to get involved with dissections, mixing tinctures, and various other aspects of her research. One afternoon as I dissected a seaworm, I wondered if she resented being replaced.

Almost as if she'd read my mind, Kalani said, "Although I dedicated my life to medicine and love treating the people of my sirene, I find I also have a passion for research. Discovering new and better treatments for diseases and injuries is really exciting. And here in my lab no one bothers me and I do what I want, when I want. It suits me." Her gentle smile crinkled the corners of her eyes; a tendril of grey-brown hair escaped the bun at the back of her head and floated around her face. I felt fortunate to be learning from her.

As she continued, I found that Kalani enjoyed our time together as much as I did. "The merkids today aren't interested in learning the old ways and sometimes call me a witch. It's sad to think that when I'm gone, no one will remember the things that used to be so natural. I'm *glad* you have such a curiosity and desire to learn about natural ways of healing. I really enjoy our afternoon sessions. You soak up information and encourage me to share what I've learned throughout my life—I now feel my efforts are worthwhile."

To treat diseases, Kalani used natural herbs and minerals found in shells, shellfish, corals, fish, kelp, sponges, worms, and other types of sea life. She willingly imparted her knowledge to me and I eagerly absorbed everything she said.

Kalani then mentioned that Dr. Nathan was very different from the old doctor. "Dr. Maldon was determined to use only what he'd been taught in school and was extremely set in his ways. He pooh-poohed my ideas and suggestions, calling them old wives' tales. Dr. Nathan is much more open to natural treatments. In fact, on a couple of occasions, he has asked me to help with a patient's particularly puzzling symptoms."

She turned to face me. "I have something to ask you, my dear. Would you mind if I invited Dr. Nathan to join us for our afternoon sessions? I think we would all benefit from learning from each other. What do you think?"

"I think it's a great idea, Kalani! As the sirene doctor, Nathan should have as many methods of healing available to him as possible. There's no such thing as too *much* knowledge." And, on a personal note, I was thrilled at the prospect of spending even *more* time with him.

The next day during our morning swim, Nathan mentioned Kalani's invitation to join our afternoon seminars. He was afraid of intruding but my broad smile and enthusiastic "Please come!" convinced him otherwise.

I loved our long swims together, the time we spent in comfortable silence just enjoying the natural beauty surrounding us, his quick smile and twinkling eyes, and knew I was seriously attracted to him. I wanted to drown in the depths of those green eyes and feel his strong arms holding me close. I often awoke from nocturnal dreams, wanting him, aching to feel his lips devouring mine. Nathan had been the consummate gentleman on our long morning swims and sometimes I wondered if he wasn't attracted to me. But once in a while, I'd catch him staring at me intently with a smoldering heat and he'd look quickly away as though caught doing something he shouldn't. At those times, I was sure he felt the same way. He would often take my hand in his during our swims and I longed for more.

I floated into Kalani's lab one afternoon and found Nathan chatting comfortably with her. A thrill ran up my spine at the prospect of our working and learning side-by-side. Hours passed quickly as Kalani happily shared her knowledge. We dissected various creatures, made poultices, and discussed what would best ease symptoms of certain diseases. We asked numerous questions and Kalani answered with what she knew. Nathan also shared his knowledge of the new ways of healing with Kalani and me, so I was learning twice as much as before.

With both of them checking regularly on my bruise and my arm, I felt I was getting the best possible care. They agreed the bruise was fading to a terrific shade of green and should disappear altogether in another week or so. The arm, however, would take longer to heal. I realized that it took longer for injuries to mend here in the ocean depths. Normally, the bruise and broken arm would have healed by now. Perhaps it had something to do with the water pressure. I didn't care how long it took, especially if it prevented Tinami and Saya from making a fateful decision. More and more, I felt I belonged here.

Early one evening, as I relaxed in my cubicle following dinner and another day spent swimming and studying with Nathan, I heard a sound at my door. Expecting to see Kiki or Maia, I glanced up to find a voluptuous, dark-haired mermaid studying me with narrowed eyes and an openly hostile demeanor. Her silvery tail deepened to sapphire then to a shocking violet at the end, a color I hadn't seen before.

Without being invited in, the woman swam boldly to the center of the room and looked me over with barely concealed disdain. Her gaze lingered on my legs and then moved to the cast on my arm. Obviously agitated, she swished from left to right and back again, never taking her eyes off me. I felt palpable waves of hate emanating from her and wondered what I could possibly have done to cause such strong feelings in someone I didn't know. She began to speak, her words measured and deliberate, her voice low and threatening.

"You spend a lot of time with Nathan and I see how you look at him. You…you with no tail and no knowledge of our ways. You think you can come here and take him from me." She lifted her chin and stared down her nose at me, haughty and suddenly motionless. The abrupt change from constant movement to total stillness unnerved me. "When his two mourning years are over, he will be married to *me*, so don't expect your helplessness to bind him to you."

At my shocked expression, she sneered. "Obviously, he hasn't told you he's promised to me. Our laws prohibit him from marrying sooner or he would already be mine." Through clenched teeth, she hissed, "You'd be wise to distance yourself before I show you how ruthless a mermaid can be."

She whirled and snapped her muscular tail. The ensuing wave nearly washed me off the bed when she darted out the door, her evil laughter fading into the distance.

Shaken, I sat, trembling with a myriad of emotions and replaying the ugly scene in my mind. I was so furious at the woman's audacity in barging into my room and threatening me that I jumped up and paced back and forth across the small space. In fact, my actions closely mirrored hers of moments before.

Then the anger was replaced by a deep hurt. I stopped pacing and pondered why Nathan hadn't told me he was promised to another. But, in his defense, he hadn't lied to me, either. And he'd never made inappropriate overtures that would indicate he was free to do so.

But how could he *not* tell me? He *had* to see my feelings clearly displayed in my eyes and on my face. He *had* to feel it whenever he held my hand.

Suddenly terror clenched my gut and I stiffened. *What would happen if the woman carried out her threat? Would she come to my room again and physically attack me? Could she poison me, leaving me to die in my bed, unable to call for help?*

Another fear intruded on my thoughts. *What would happen if this was brought to Tinami and Saya's attention? Would I be sent away and Nathan forced to marry this awful woman?* That was the most unbearable idea of all.

The strength left my legs and I collapsed on the edge of the bed. Here, in this mermaid-driven society, the women were the providers; they pursued their chosen mates. Tinami and Saya might see the woman's actions as totally justifiable. Not a permanent resident of this sirene, I had only been accepted as a temporary guest until my injuries healed. Surprisingly, no one had broached the subject of returning me to the surface in the months I'd been here. But if Tinami and Saya examined this situation closely, I would undoubtedly be asked to leave. What would I do? Where would I go? How would I survive? No doubt I would perish if sent away.

Hopeless, drained, I slid from the bed to the floor and puddled in a boneless heap. Sobs wracked my body while copious tears merged invisibly with the saltwater; my sore, swollen eyes could see only heartbreak and disaster ahead. I desperately needed to talk to Nathan, but couldn't risk calling attention to our relationship by seeking him out tonight. In spite of needing him so dreadfully, I decided to wait until the next morning when we could talk during our swim, far from the prying eyes and ears of the sirene.

CHAPTER 5

MAIA STOPPED BY later that same evening for a short visit. Although I had pulled myself together, I couldn't enjoy her company with such a heavy heart. I apologized and told her I didn't feel well. "Maybe we should do this another time." We chatted a few minutes more and she jokingly suggested I see Dr. Nathan.

I felt guilty for not being more open with her, but I hadn't seen much of Maia recently and I didn't want too many people to know about my feelings for Nathan. She left with a promise to come by more often. "Take care of yourself. I'll visit another time."

That night, I tossed and turned restlessly, plagued by unpleasant dreams I couldn't quite recall in the light of day. I barely tasted my breakfast, my stomach tied in knots and my nerves jangling. Afterwards, I paced back and forth across my tiny cubicle, both dreading and anticipating Nathan's appearance at my door.

When he finally poked his head into the cubicle, he knew at first glance that something was wrong. I'm sure my serious countenance and muttered, "We can talk outside," didn't reassure him. We swam in silence to the cavern opening and

Nathan performed his chivalrous predator check at the doorway.

Some distance away, I turned to face him. My face contorted as I fought back tears. I didn't even know where to begin this most difficult of conversations, especially since my voice was shaky with emotion.

He took my hand and murmured, "Come."

The delay gave me the opportunity to regain my composure so when Nathan stopped at the entrance to a small cave, I was a bit calmer. He checked inside and then motioned for me to enter. At the back of the cave a pile of rock provided a natural seating area and we settled to talk. Nathan reached for my hand, but for the first time I pulled away. His touch would make it that much more difficult to talk about his relationship with another woman.

The only way to begin was to begin. "I had a visitor last night. A woman who said that once your two years of mourning are over, she will marry you. I..." My voice broke. I couldn't continue and glanced up to see Nathan's reaction.

He looked broken, defeated. I wanted to reach out and hold him but had to know the truth. Finally, he took a deep breath, met my eyes, and began a story that I needed, hated, had to hear.

"I told you part of the story the day you asked me about Saralee. You know I've always been different from other mermen and why I refused to mate early in life."

I nodded, afraid to reply for fear my voice would betray my inner turmoil.

He paused, collecting his thoughts, and I could tell this was difficult for him so I kept silent.

"As I mentioned before, we had only been married for several months when Saralee didn't return from that hunting expedition." He paused and lowered his head, turning his eyes away from mine. When he continued, his voice was rough with emotion and I fought the urge to touch him.

"The hunting party had seen the shark's tell-tale danger signs and turned as a group to head in the other direction. A young, inexperienced woman was watching something on the sea floor and didn't realize everyone had moved off. Others in the group said Saralee glanced back and saw the girl swim forward a few more feet, just enough to be well inside the shark's territory. He made a tight circle then sped toward the girl who was still unaware of the danger. Saralee darted into the shark's view to divert his attention." He swallowed hard and finally raised his face to mine.

My heart clenched at the raw pain in his eyes, the tightness of his jaw.

"The shark attacked, giving the girl time to swim back to the group."

Nathan once again averted his eyes and his voice hardened. "Saralee's older sister is the woman who visited you last night. The women couldn't have been more different: Saralee was blonde, gentle, and caring while Valkar is dark-haired, bold, selfish, and has a heart as black as night. Sirene law decrees that I take my dead wife's sister as mate, if she's unwed, as soon as the two-year mourning is over. In six months, I'm supposed to marry Valkar and begin having children soon after. The thought of living out my life with that devil-woman makes my skin crawl."

He shivered. Then he turned his glance back to me. His voice and eyes softened and his hands clasped mine a bit tighter. "Then you took my breath away that day outside the common room. I literally couldn't speak."

I recalled that moment when our bodies collided, how I got lost during that first glance into his beautiful green eyes.

His voice brought me back to the present. "You're so different from the mermaids. You're hungry for knowledge, to learn our ways, to contribute to our society even though it's different from anything you've previously known. You have passion for life and live every moment with joy." His eyes bored into mine with an intensity that made me blush. His lips curled at the corners as though a smile awaited but his words rushed out in a breathy torrent instead.

"When we swim together, it's all I can do to keep from bringing you here and making you mine...in every way. At first, I fought the attraction, knowing I was promised to Valkar. In addition, you were only supposed to stay until your injuries healed, and our laws forbid us from going to the surface. How can we return you safely?" He moved even closer, pulling me toward him until there were only inches separating us.

"After a while, all I could think of was our morning swim, your smile, the feel of your hand in mine, and I knew I'd found the love I'd always wanted. But how could I act on those feelings when I belong to another? Even if I despise her? The sirene would evict us both, send you away and force me to marry Valkar, or put you to death—all are impossible!" Momentarily, he squeezed his eyes shut and took a deep, shuddering breath.

When he looked once more into my eyes, the raw emotion on his face tore at my heart. I felt his pain, his love, his need for understanding and reassurance. I reached up to touch his face and found myself in his arms, our lips meeting for the first time. His mouth claimed mine, softly insistent at first and then becoming more demanding as our passion flared. We'd kept it restrained for so long that there was no holding back.

Briefly, I wondered if our bodies would meld, woman to merman. Hands, mouths, tongues, that beautiful cleft in Nathan's chin that I had lusted after from day one...nothing was out of bounds. I found it terribly erotic to slide my hand down his strong, beautiful tail as he wrapped it around my lower body. Holding me close to him with that tail, his hands explored every inch of me and I found a merman makes love in much the same way a human man does.

As I explored his body with eager hands, I discovered a pouch on his belly that blended perfectly into his skin; tail-scales just brushed the bottom edge. It softened and opened and I slid my hand inside. From his reaction, I realized this was a very sensitive area.

Hungry to feel him touching me, too, I unzipped my Lycra wetskin and slithered out of it, tossing the bathing suit and fins aside, as well. Nathan pulled me close, skin on skin, as we knelt in the soft sand, his lips moving hungrily from my mouth to my shoulders, leaving fiery trails in the wake of his kisses.

Although mermaids are physically different than human women, Nathan quickly learned how to pleasure me. But still, I wanted more. We had denied ourselves for so long that I couldn't wait and Nathan's passion equaled mine as we lay back in the sand. We soon found a rhythm that further aroused us both and my nails dug into Nathan's back as his tail whipped up the sand in the small cave.

Afterwards, arms, legs, and tail intertwined, we snuggled, catching our breath and murmuring endearments, our hands gently caressing each other in the afterglow. The sand settled softly around us as though we reclined in a snow globe.

"You have an amazingly gentle and erotic touch, Two-Tails. You make me crazy. That was absolutely amazing."

"And you figured out how to make love to a two-tails pretty quickly. Are you sure I'm the first human you've ever been with?" Even though I had buried my face against Nathan's chest, the teasing tone in my voice reached his ears.

"Well, there was a blonde several years ago… OUCH!" I poked him in the ribs and he squeezed me tightly in a hug. His whispered reply melted my heart. "There has *never* been anyone like you in my life." He tilted my chin up to gaze lovingly into my eyes. "And there will never *be* anyone else. You are the love and passion that I've longed for."

We lay tangled on the cave floor, completely engrossed in finally expressing our love for each other. Eventually, though, we knew we needed to return to the cavern. I felt that everyone who saw me would know I was head over heels in love. I took his hand and pulled him close to voice my concerns.

"Nathan, how do I hide my feelings for you? Especially now that we've been together like this. My emotions are always written all over my face and everyone will know. I'm afraid I'll say or do something and the wrong person will suspect the truth. I don't know if I can do this."

I sobbed as Nathan reassured me. His soft voice eventually calmed my fears. "We'll go about our routine as normally as possible until we figure out what to do. We always swim at 10:00 and then spend the afternoon with Kalani. The mermaids are out foraging most of the day and they're the ones who would most likely recognize your feelings. Just try to stay calm."

His logic made perfect sense—if only I could wear a mask to hide my emotions.

"It'll be okay. I promise, it'll be okay."

I wanted to believe him, but so many things could go wrong. And I hoped Valkar didn't pay me any more visits. I *knew* I couldn't handle *that*.

CHAPTER 6

EVERY MORNING, Nathan would come to my cubicle and we'd nonchalantly exit the cavern Once out of sight, we'd swim quickly to our little cave to be alone. We made love frequently, reveling in discovering every inch of each other's body, learning how to bring the other as much pleasure as possible, falling more and more in love with each passing day.

Sometimes we'd lie in each other's arms and discuss what we'd do if evicted from the sirene, how we'd begin a new life together. We tried not to dwell on the possibility that we could be put to death rather than exiled. That was too morbid to think about when we were so joyously in love.

In between discussing potential plans and enjoying our new-found love, Nathan finally removed the cast from my arm. It seemed to have healed perfectly but he wanted me to be careful for a while, to avoid re-injury. With the cast gone and the bruise on my forehead a thing of the past, I was nearly back to normal. I hoped it wouldn't prompt Tinami and Saya to make a fateful decision.

I had been toying with the idea of asking Nathan to teach me to hunt and forage for food, a skill I would desperately need if banished. Besides, if I was a useful, contributing member, perhaps Tinami and Saya would be more lenient and allow me to stay indefinitely. However, with Nathan's admonishment to be careful with my now-cast-less arm, I figured I ought to wait a while before bringing it up.

Days, then weeks went by, and we maintained our regular morning swims followed by afternoon seminars with Kalani. I managed to preserve an air of normalcy in spite of my inner turmoil and spending time with Kalani helped since I didn't have to pretend around her. But one day when Nathan and I arrived for our seminar, she wore a frown and greeted us with an unusually somber demeanor. When Nathan asked if everything was alright, Kalani shook her head and sighed sadly.

"I overheard Tinami and Saya discussing Serena and what should be done. Everyone has noticed the amount of time you two spend together and the daily swims can no longer be labeled physical therapy. They feel it's inappropriate since you're supposed to be marrying Valkar in only four months. And Serena's not even a mermaid. They called your behavior disgraceful. I'm afraid for the two of you." The worry showed plainly in her eyes and frown lines furrowed deeply into her forehead.

Kalani knew that Nathan and I were in love—the glow emanating from the two of us was unmistakable. But Kalani was too much of a friend and a professional to mention it.

Nathan and I exchanged a telling glance and I knew we needed to be completely open and honest with her. He understood my intent, nodded slightly, and filled her in on our plans, his voice simultaneously determined and anxious.

"Kalani, we value your friendship and love you dearly. We want you to know what we've been talking about, the decision we've made. We want to leave the sirene and strike out on our own to make a new nest. With time growing short in my two years of mourning, I'll soon be forced to marry Valkar. And I can't! She threatened Serena verbally about a month ago and we're afraid she might act on her jealousy. If she hurts Serena, I don't know what I'll do." Nathan turned to look at me and the love in his eyes made my heart swell with joy.

He continued his plea. "The situation has become impossible—we *can't* stay here. Yes, it's dangerous to leave, but we love each other and it's the only way we can be together. We feel it's even *more* dangerous to stay." We clasped hands and faced her, desperate. "Will you help us?"

Wringing her hands and leaning back against the countertop with a frown marring her usually gentle countenance, Kalani voiced her thoughts. "Valkar has always been a troublemaker. No one in the sirene trusts her and it would be just like her to physically attack someone who stands in the way of what she wants. We tolerated her for many years because Saralee was so well-liked—kind of like taking the good with the bad. But now the good is gone and Valkar is out of control. She has no positive guiding influence." She paused then plunged ahead with her deepest concerns.

"You both realize, don't you, that your chances of survival are minimal with only the two of you to keep each other safe? Serena, you aren't a mermaid. You've never been taught how to hunt, forage, and provide for your family. When you have a child and Nathan has to stay behind to care for him, how will you protect and feed them? There's safety in numbers and much risk for only two."

I spoke up, determined, sounding much calmer than I felt. "Kalani, we have no choice. We *can't* stay here. I will *learn* how to provide for and protect my family—because I *have* to! Please help us?"

Kalani pulled us both close in a tearful hug. "Of course, I'll help you in any way I can!"

CHAPTER 7

THEN NATHAN BROUGHT me astonishing news. One morning, as soon as we reached our little cave, he took my hands and sat me down to talk. "My love, I have something to tell you and I'm not sure how you'll react. I'm…we're pregnant. We're having a child.

He stopped, seeing my shocked expression. I was stunned. Thrilled. Terrified…and totally confused. How…? Well, I knew *how* it had happened, sort of, but wasn't prepared for the fact that it *had*. "How…? When…? What will we…?"

At my stammering response, he explained. "I'll carry the baby inside a sac behind my pouch for five months. Then, the fetus will slip into the pouch, here…" He placed our hands together on his belly. "… for the last month. After that, it will remain in the pouch but will be free to explore outside as it grows. Eventually, he…she…will leave the pouch altogether."

My mind was in a whirl and the confusion must have shown on my face. "How does this work, Nathan? How did *you* get pregnant when I carry the egg? How does it work with mermaids and mermen? I'm completely confused."

Nathan simplified the mermaid reproduction process and explained so I could understand. "When a mermaid is ovulating, she provides an egg that is extracted from her body into the male's penis during sex. Lovemaking creates enough suction that the egg is sucked into a tube where it travels to a sac located behind the pouch. When the male's body detects the presence of a viable egg, sperm is ejaculated into the sac and washes over the egg, fertilizing it. It embeds itself into the lining of the sac where it gains nutrients from the male's body."

Incredulity had to show plainly on my face, but Nathan patiently continued his explanation. "When we made love, it must have worked about the same way. Even though your body is externally different from a mermaid's, the internal parts are evidently very similar. During ovulation, our lovemaking must have created enough suction to extract an egg from your body. Once the egg was deposited in my sac, the process was the same. I provided the sperm that fertilized the egg—and now we're pregnant."

My head swam with the news, thoughts whirling in my mind. Was it miraculous or tragic that our bodies had found a way to reproduce in the face of such a challenging situation? How could we leave the sirene and live on our own if Nathan was pregnant? How would I learn to forage, hunt, and defend my family? There was so much I didn't know about providing and protecting, and yet we couldn't very well remain in the cavern and have him marry Valkar, pregnant with our child.

Once the news was out, I was sure to be evicted—alone—or, and this thought made my blood run cold, put to death. It was an unbearable situation.

We decided to talk to Kalani that afternoon. Perhaps she would have a suggestion.

After we broke the news, Kalani wept. "I love you both, individually and as a couple, and I can't see any way this can have a happy ending. I wish I could change things so you could stay here and be my family. I'll try to think of something." Her anguished cry tore at my heart.

Nathan and I continued our daily routine, afraid to do anything differently. We swam, made love, and talked. But it was hard to make plans or get excited about our coming child when everything was so uncertain. Any day, I expected to be summoned to Tinami and Saya for my eviction notice... Yet nothing happened.

With all my inner turmoil, I needed an outlet for the anxiety that was eating me up. I decided to broach the subject of learning to hunt and forage on one of our swims.

"Nathan, I've been thinking... Can you teach me how to hunt and forage? Now that my arm has healed, I have to do *something* or I'll go crazy. I'll need those skills once we leave the sirene and now is the perfect time for me to learn—when our lives don't depend on my success."

He stopped swimming and cocked his head slightly, a small frown creasing his forehead. I could see him processing my request. I held my breath, wondering how he'd answer.

"My dear Two-Tails, I love you for wanting to learn those skills and I agree, now would be the best time. But the mermaids are the most proficient hunters. Even as a merkid, as you recall, I was more interested in shadowing the doctor than in playing hunting games with the other kids. I'd be a lousy teacher even if we had all the time in the world. I'm sorry."

My face fell and I looked away in disappointment.

He hugged me and we continued our swim. I mentally made a vow to come up with another way of learning the skills I would so desperately need.

Another month went by and during our lovemaking one morning, I noticed Nathan's belly looked bigger—he was starting to show. Surely someone would suspect why and then all hell would break loose. More stressed than I'd ever been, I felt I could fall apart at any moment. Kalani remarked on my emotional state when I arrived early one afternoon for our seminar.

"How are you holding up, dear? You seem very much on edge."

Her caring concern set me babbling, the words coming out in a torrent. "Oh, Kalani, if we don't do something soon I'll go out of my mind! Yesterday, I was so preoccupied I swam right past my room; my stomach is in knots and I have trouble eating; sleep is nearly impossible."

I took a ragged breath and continued, jabbering even faster. "Nathan's starting to show and someone is going to notice and then I'm going to be evicted and he'll have to marry Valkar and…and…" I dissolved into a tearful, hiccupping mess, trembling and wailing as Kalani wrapped her bony arms around me.

She made soothing noises and stroked my hair. Eventually, the torrent subsided and I apologized. "I'm so sorry, Kalani. I guess I've bottled my emotions up and just needed to release some of the stress." I felt better for having vented and by the time Nathan arrived for our session, Kalani and I were chatting as though nothing had happened. I didn't want him to know how I'd fallen apart. It would only worry him more.

Maia visited me one evening several days later and she, also, noticed how jittery I was. At her concerned tone and fond look, I burst out sobbing again. Once the floodgates opened, I couldn't seem to stop and told her the whole story, holding nothing back. She put her arms around me, but her consoling hug had little effect.

"I feel guilty for bringing you into the sirene to begin with. If it wasn't for me, you wouldn't be in this mess!"

I wailed back, "Maia, I don't blame you for any of this. If you hadn't found me and brought me here, I'd be dead!" and then we realized how ridiculous we sounded.

We traded wan smiles and Maia asked, "What are you going to do? It seems like such an utterly hopeless situation. I agree that your only chance of being together is to leave the cavern, but even that doesn't seem like a great solution. How will you survive on your own? With a baby?"

At her last comment I recalled my suggestion to Nathan and another idea sprang to life. "Maia, I have an idea. Would you teach me to hunt and find food like you do for the sirene? I'll need that knowledge once Nathan and I leave and he's not skilled enough to teach me. It needs to be a mermaid—you'd be perfect for the job! What do you think?"

She thought about it for a long moment. "We'd have to hunt after I get back from foraging with the other mermaids, later in the afternoons. As long as I don't neglect my other responsibilities, I think it would be fine. You'll definitely need those skills if you and Nathan go off on your own."

I was thrilled and agreed with her timeline. "I usually meet with Kalani and Nathan every afternoon, but I could go out with you three times a week instead. Kalani and Nathan would know what we were doing but no one else would miss me since I'm always occupied at that time, anyway. What do you think? Would it work? Would anyone object?"

We grinned at each other. Maia was enthusiastic. "Of course it'll work! And I don't know why anyone would object to you learning something that would ultimately benefit the sirene—no one needs to know you have an ulterior motive. Let's start on Monday. That'll give me three days to decide what you'll need to know first, where to go for our sessions, and how best to teach you. We can meet at Kalani's lab at 3:00 and can come and go through her private entrance." She stayed a while longer and then we hugged at the door.

I prepared for bed, climbed under the covers, and snuggled into my little nest, more relaxed than I'd been in a long while. I had a plan! Soon, I dozed off, free of the nightmares and anxiety that had plagued my sleep for the last few weeks.

Suddenly, I jerked awake to a rough hand covering my mouth and nose with a foul-tasting rag. A muscular body pinned me down. The thick darkness effectively blinded me so I couldn't see my attacker, but her strength and weight indicated a mermaid. In my terror, I howled into the rag and beat at her with useless fists. All too soon, my brain went fuzzy and my leaden arms fell limp at my sides. As my eyes rolled back in my head, my mind screamed, "Nathan! Help me!"

CHAPTER 8

SMALL, SHARP-EDGED ROCKS poked into my back, like bony fingers digging into my skin. I shifted, vaguely wondering why my bed had stones in it. My head throbbed and I tried to hold it still, hoping the pain would subside. My mouth felt fuzzy.

As I tried to sit up, weak and disoriented, the terror of the attack rushed back. Gasping and trying to see into the darkness, I struggled to my feet, reeling with dizziness. *Was she still there?* My heart pounded, the only noise I could hear in the enveloping silence.

When my straining ears heard nothing, I slowly sank back onto the sparse bunk, realizing I was no longer in my room. I listened intently, trying to discern where I might be and if someone else was nearby. I didn't know which would be worse: to be totally alone in the darkness or to be blind in the darkness, *not* alone. I whimpered, the sound small and sad in the muffled blackness.

Nothing moved. No one spoke. I curled up in a ball and tried my best to disappear.

***

I had no idea how long I lay there. Hours? Days? My muscles ached and yearned to stretch. Nothing stirred in the thick darkness. I slowly sat, then stood, the effects of the drug having worn off. Warily, I took a few small steps forward, reaching overhead and in front of me with outstretched arms, feeling each step cautiously with my feet. When I encountered nothing above, on the floor, or in front of me, I took a few more steps. The third time, my hand met vertical bars running from the floor as high up as I could reach. Using the bars to pull myself up, the water aiding my buoyancy, I found they securely met a metal ceiling. I then followed the bars from one side of the room to the other and visualized a metal box in the darkness.

Fighting a bout of claustrophobia, I forced myself to sit and breathe, to think. *Who would do this? Why would they do this?*

Valkar! She had threatened to show me how ruthless a mermaid could be. I doubted food would be provided; surely, I'd be left here alone to die.

Rather than dwell on the worst that could happen, I explored the cell. It didn't take long. It was empty save for the crude bunk composed of rocks and a thin layer of kelp. With no idea how far I was from the cavern, it was pointless to hope the next day's hunting party might stumble upon my prison. I fought to remain calm and lay back on the uncomfortable bed, focusing my thoughts on Nathan, his smile, and those incredible green eyes. I allowed my mind to drift and recalled the hours we'd spent swimming together.

Time crawled as I drifted in and out of sleep, trying to envision a happy ending to the situation. Hunger and stress took their toll. Darkness was total when the sun set, but during daylight hours the cell lightened to a murky, gun-metal grey. I realized I was imprisoned in a sunken ship when I saw a narrow hall extending past the bars, another cell directly opposite mine.

The only light filtered in through the wreckage. How long the wreck had lain here, I had no idea. Surely years considering the barnacles and the amount of coral growing on nearly all surfaces.

Fish swam leisurely up and down the hall and between the bars and I attempted to catch one. Although the thought of biting into a still-living, still-moving fish turned my empty stomach, it would be nourishment I desperately needed. However, I wasn't quick enough and the potential meals mocked me as they swam freely in and out of my prison.

Well after sunset on what I thought was the third night, I lay on the rocky bed and finally faced the fact that I would die here in this lonely cell. Recalling what I'd been told about humans being able to exist underwater as long as they were near mer-people, I began to wonder how long I could survive alone. Would I slowly starve to death? Or would I eventually drown now that I was no longer under the somewhat magical influence of the sirene?

Fear and claustrophobia nearly drove me mad as I panicked, futilely pounding on the bars with bruised and aching fists, howling my fear and hopelessness into the darkness. Weakness overcame me and I staggered to the crude bunk. Knowing Nathan would be out of his mind with worry, I curled up into a ball, hugging my knees to my chest, and pictured his dear face. I needed something to clear my mind, to keep total despair at bay. I couldn't just give up.

Eventually, I composed myself and sat on the edge of the bed, slowing my racing heart and regulating my breathing. A plan—I needed a plan.

Years ago, I had taken a meditation class and found it very helpful in reducing stress and focusing my thoughts. If ever I needed to relax and focus, it was now. Recalling every step in the process, I pictured Nathan in my mind, concentrating on his face, our love, our child. I closed my eyes. Taking long, slow, deep breaths, clearing my mind of anything but Nathan, I centered myself and held him and our love foremost in my thoughts. With no distractions, surrounded by darkness and total silence, I found myself going deeper than I ever had before. I sat like that until time became irrelevant, my thoughts and the force of my love directed at Nathan like a beam of light.

My eyelids fluttered open and I saw my body sitting on the edge of the bed, deep in meditation. I looked around and realized I hovered near the ceiling, gazing down at myself. I'd never had an out-of-body experience but had read of others who described the phenomenon. I felt calm, peaceful even, the terror and despair of earlier totally absent.

Not knowing how long I could remain in this state or what might happen if my body was disturbed while I was away, forced me to take action. I approached the bars and reached out to touch them, only slightly surprised when my hand passed through like they didn't exist. I swam out of the cell, through the walls of the wreckage, and into open water.

In my concentration, I had directed my thoughts at Nathan like a beam of light. Now, in the inky vastness of dark ocean water, I clearly saw a luminous shaft of glimmering light leading off to my left and disappearing into the distance. I swam toward it, stopping where it seemed to begin. I reached into the lightbeam and my hand sparkled and glowed. I smiled, comforted by the warm, soothing sensation.

Suddenly, a movement caught my eye. I whirled to the right, my heart racing. Dolphins! There were at least ten of the beautiful, sleek creatures surrounding me.

One stopped directly in front of me and looked deep into my eyes. I was mesmerized by her soothing, hypnotic gaze.

Tingly tendrils nudged into my mind and I opened my thoughts and emotions, allowing her to enter. In my mind, I heard her say, "Hello, Serena, I've felt your desperation for some time now but couldn't help until you allowed me in. Your spirit and mine have met. Grasp my fin and I will lead you home."

Excited clicks and sonar whistles came from all directions as she turned and offered me her back. I grasped her dorsal fin with both hands and she swam slowly, directly into the lightbeam. Astonished, I saw dolphins arrayed on either side of us, the two in front clearly lit and shimmering in the glow of the beam's luminescence. A feeling of being wrapped in love and warmth stole over me and I understood the beam was the manifestation of the love I felt for Nathan.

We sailed effortlessly through the water and before long, I spied the entrance to the cavern. As the dolphins came to a stop, the female turned and looked me in the eye again. She nodded, bobbing her head toward the cavern opening. I heard her speak in my mind. "Hurry. We will wait for you here." The other dolphins slowly circled the cave mouth.

I floated in through the fissure, swam around the bend, and saw a flurry of activity, mermaids and mermen darting to and fro, concern apparent in their movements. I saw Maia and eagerly swam over to greet her, but she ignored me. I spoke again and then realized she couldn't see or hear me. With a sinking heart, I wondered how I could summon help. And would Nathan be able to hear me?

Heading to his quarters, I briefly wondered if the close proximity of the mer-people to my spirit would be sufficient to sustain me until my body could return to the sirene.

As I passed a group of mermaids, I overheard Tinami discussing an organized search of the connecting cave system. I paused to listen. Nathan had notified Tinami and Saya of my absence, but at first they thought I might have been exploring the adjoining small caves and lost my bearings. When more time had passed, they came to believe I may have been injured and was unable to call for help. They had already thoroughly combed the main cavern and all cubicles. If nothing was found in the connecting system, another group of mermaids was planning to expand the quest outside in the morning.

Their plan sounded plausible, but I knew the search would yield nothing. I darted away and found Nathan sitting on a pile of soft sand in the corner of his room, sobbing, hands clasped over his slightly swollen belly. He bowed his head and I saw his lips moving. I floated closer and made out his desperate plea.

"Please, please, help me find her. She's the most precious thing in my life and I can't lose her. I'll do anything if I can only have her back. Please…"

I realized he was praying. Kneeling in front of him, emotional, I said, "Nathan, I'm here. I'm here."

His lips stopped moving and he cocked his head as though listening.

I spoke again. "I'm here and I need your help."

He looked around the room, confusion and uncertainty on his face.

"Nathan, concentrate on our love; hold it close in your mind. I'm here."

He closed his eyes and I could feel his breathing slow. I gently touched his hand and his eyes flew open.

"Serena?"

"Yes, Nathan, I'm here! You can't see me because i'm… Oh, I can't explain it. We have to go. Can you hear me?"

"Yes, sort of—you're a faint whisper in my mind. I don't understand. Tell me what you need."

"We have to leave the cavern. Quickly."

Nathan darted to the doorway and headed toward the entrance. "Serena? Should we bring others?" He looked around, concentrating on my voice.

"Yes, bring five strong mermaids. And tools of some sort—pry bars. We'll need them." I watched as he called to the others to gather round and sent the youngest to fetch Tinami.

"Everyone! I need your attention. Serena needs our help. Five of the strongest mermaids, grab the sturdiest bone pry bars you can find and meet me at the cavern entrance right away. Hurry!"

Tinami swam up to Nathan, listened to his explanation, and although his face registered puzzled disbelief, he nodded in agreement. They waited together as the mermaids scattered and reassembled at the cavern door, tools in hand. Nathan led the way outside where everyone stopped in shock at sight of the dolphins waiting just beyond the opening and the shimmering beam of light leading into the darkness.

"Good luck," Tinami said, "and be careful. Bring Serena back safely."

The female dolphin swam up, turned, and stopped so I could again grasp her dorsal fin. As we swam into the lightbeam, I heard Nathan say, "Serena! I can see you in the shimmering light! This is amazing!"

We swam hard and fast back to the wreck. The sun would soon rise and I feared the lightbeam would disappear in the daylight.

Just as darkness began to fade into grey, we arrived at the ship. My dolphin stopped to let me off and turned again to look me in the eye. I stroked her side and our minds met again.

I smiled. *Thank you. You saved my life.*

I could swear she smiled back as she bobbed her head and whistled to the pod. They darted away, quickly disappearing into the grey-blue water, and I heard her thoughts once more. "You're welcome, Serena. You can call to me any time—use the power of your mind."

Although reluctant to return to that awful prison, I swam into the opening and down the hall with the others following. As before, I passed easily through the bars and approached my body sitting on the edge of the bed, just as I'd left it. From about six inches away, I felt a slight tug at the core of my being and merged with my physical self.

I looked up, straining to see Nathan and the mermaids through the murky grey-blackness. Crowded in the hallway, studying the bars, the mermaids searched for the weakest point.

Nathan reached through the bars to grab my hand. "Serena! I have no idea what's going on but I'm *so* happy to see you! Now, back away from the doorway while we pry the bars loose. We'll get you out of there."

And with five strong mermaids wielding the heavy bone pry bars, I was soon free and safely back in Nathan's arms.

CHAPTER 9

NIGHT SURRENDERED EASILY to the light of day as we found our way back to the cavern. We entered the opening and paused at the overhead ledge. I saw the entire sirene clustered around the leaders, anxiously awaiting our return. Tinami had told everyone that Nathan had led the group to rescue me and they were all eager to hear about the dolphins and the extraordinary beam of light.

Hands reached out to touch me as we swam toward Tinami and Saya. Voices called out. "Are you alright? What happened?" "What was that light? Where'd it come from?" "Did you talk to the dolphins?"

Finally, we stopped in front of the leaders. Saya smiled, rose, and gave me a sincere hug. Tinami then took my hands in both of his and said warmly, "Welcome back, Serena. We're all glad you're safe."

I nodded and smiled broadly, thankful to be home.

He continued. "I'm sure you have an amazing story to tell, but you need rest, food, and time to settle your nerves. The story can wait. Tonight there will be a special dinner in the common room so everyone can attend—you can regale us all with your remarkable tale then. Go, now."

Tinami ordered Nathan to check me over to be sure there were no lasting effects from the ordeal. The throng parted as we swam slowly out of the main cavern on our way to my room. I turned my head to speak to Nathan, saw a quick movement at the edge of the crowd, and instinctively stiffened as I recognized Valkar's long black hair and shockingly violet tail. I gasped at the brazen hate on her face. Her narrowed eyes shot daggers at my heart right before she disappeared around a wall. I knew she had orchestrated my abduction and planned to let me die in that cell. *With this scheme thwarted what would she do next?*

When we reached my cubicle, Nathan wrapped his arms around me and held me so tightly I could hardly breathe. "I'm so thankful you're safe. I don't know what I would've done…" His voice broke and my heart constricted.

"Nathan, I'm fine. Please, let me breathe."

He loosened his hold, looked into my face, and smiled tenderly. He was so shaken by the incident, I couldn't bring Valkar's name up just yet—I was afraid of what he might do.

"I'm exhausted and hungry. Can you please give me a quick once-over? Maybe by then the food will arrive."

"I'm sorry, Serena. I'll get you a snack first; we'll do the physical afterwards. Sit here." I sat on the edge of the bed while Nathan swam off. He had only been gone a minute when a servant arrived with my meal. I ate with gusto and Nathan found me in a better humor when he returned. He set the snack aside in case I should want it later. We chatted as I cleaned my plate, thankful to have a full stomach again.

After a brief physical, another hug, and a few loving kisses, Nathan tucked me into bed and promised to check on me later. I would be telling my story at dinner that night and I wanted to be refreshed before launching into the tale. Nathan and I needed to discuss what details I should share. We knew who was behind the abduction and why, but we needed to decide how much I should divulge to the others.

About 2:00, Nathan returned and woke me from a sound sleep. I yawned, stretched, and smiled lovingly into his green eyes. "I'm so happy to be back. That sorry excuse for a bed was like lying on a board riddled with nails." Hugging him close, I said, "We need to decide how much information I should include in tonight's story. I don't want to say something that will make the situation worse.

"And I don't think I should mention the mind-communication with the dolphin. I don't want to be looked at as some kind of witch or animal whisperer. I need everyone's support, not suspicion, and, frankly, I couldn't explain how it happened, anyway."

He leaned back and sighed. "You're right. Exclude that part. We can go over the rest of the story repeatedly until it all makes sense."

For the next two hours we honed the tale until it sounded plausible, leaving out any reference to our intimate relationship, Valkar's involvement, and talking to the dolphin. It left a lot of questions unanswered, but I could claim to be as in the dark as everyone else. I just hoped Valkar wouldn't make a scene.

Nathan left around 4:00. With dinner scheduled for 6 p.m., I had time to relax and review the story again. Finally, I swam to the common room and found it as crowded as I'd ever seen it. The merkids were relegated to another room, several teenagers supervising their meal and after-dinner play. This banquet was for adults only.

The elegant and sumptuous buffet table tempted everyone to eat more than they should. I recognized lobster, shrimp, sea bass, clams, and oysters; salads made of various types of undersea greens; numerous vegetables; and delectable desserts.

Dinner tables wore lacy, sea fan tablecloths of pale blue and purple. Lustrous mother-of-pearl plates adorned each place setting. I had never seen such a beautiful dining room.

The mermaids had taken special care with their appearance, too, pinning hair up with shimmering shell clips and pins. Stray tendrils floated around faces carefully made up with waterproof eye shadow and lipstick; pearls of various shapes and sizes glistened at necks and wrists and dangled from earlobes like tiny opalescent bubbles. Even the mermen seemed dressed up although no suits, ties, or tuxedos made an appearance. It must have been the air of elegance and sophistication that brought out everyone's decorum. I felt extremely underdressed in my hot pink Lycra wetskin and fins.

The wait staff mingled, handing out a seemingly unending supply of hors d'oeuvres and a gnarly, sort-of-round, plump worm that everyone was consuming with gusto. I saw a few wriggle slightly as a waiter passed and wondered what it might be.

I waited at the doorway, loath to mix with this elegant crowd, until Maia spotted me.

"Serena! Come in, come in and join everyone! We're all dying to hear what happened. You *are* okay, aren't you? Whoever did this didn't hurt you?"

Shaking my head, I said, "I'm just feeling a bit underdressed and overwhelmed. I've never seen so many beautiful people in one place. And look at *you*! You're gorgeous!"

Maia beamed at the compliment just as Nathan appeared at my side. "Dinner's ready. We need to take our seats."

As we floated toward the dinner tables, he leaned into me and whispered, "I haven't seen Valkar anywhere. Hopefully, she won't show."

I flashed him a grateful smile while looking for my place card. Thankfully, Nathan and I were seated together—I didn't want to go through this ordeal without him nearby. Tinami sat at the head of the long table with Saya to his right, a royal couple, all glitz and glamour.

Once everyone was seated, Tinami made a toast. "Tonight we are thankful that Serena has been found. She is safe and back with us again. We're all anxious to hear her tale, but it will wait until after dinner. Enjoy your meal."

Everyone raised one of those gnarly-looking worms, popped it into his mouth, then rose and floated single file to the buffet table.

I turned to Nathan with a puzzled frown and whispered, "What are those awful-looking worms everyone is eating?"

He chuckled. "They're whiskey-worms. Eaten raw, they contain a high alcohol content. If everyone consumes enough, they won't even remember your story tomorrow."

Just then, Kalani swam up and gave me a heartfelt hug. "I was so worried about you, my dear. And I'm glad you're back, safe and sound." She smiled, her eyes nearly disappearing in the crinkles, and leaned in close to whisper, "Do you know who was behind this?"

I smiled back and gave her another hug, my lips near her ear. "We'll have to talk later." Unfortunately, Kalani's seat was too far away to converse during dinner and I didn't want anyone to overhear.

The meal was outstanding, but I declined to try the whiskey-worms. No one else seemed to have any self-imposed limits, though, and I thought I could probably weave a fantastic story about a magical whale and they would enjoy it without question.

As the wait staff cleared the dessert plates from the table, Tinami's personal aide hummed forcefully into the end of a large conch shell to gain everyone's attention. The ensuing sound reverberated loudly, amplified in the water, and drowned out the babble of voices. Gradually, the room fell silent.

Tinami rose and gestured in my direction. "I'm sure you are anxious to hear Serena's story. Please remain quiet until she's finished. If she's up to answering questions, she can do so then."

When Tinami took his seat all eyes turned to me. With a knot in my stomach, I stood and smiled, hoping to look and sound convincing. "First, I'd like to thank everyone for your concern and help in rescuing me. I still have a lot of questions myself, but will relate what happened as best I can.

"Three nights ago, as I slept, a mermaid attacked and abducted me. Although I couldn't see her in the darkness, I know it was a mermaid by her size and strength. She held a foul-tasting rag over my nose and mouth and I passed out. When I regained consciousness, I found myself locked in a cell in a downed ship. I had no idea where I was, who had taken me, why they had done such a thing, or when or if they would come back. For all I knew, I would die there."

I looked around the room, at the faces of people I had come to care for and felt guilty about the lie. But my life depended upon convincing everyone I didn't know who was behind the abduction or why they had done it.

My voice shook slightly as I resumed the tale. "I was terrified and knew the morning hunting party wouldn't accidentally find me. After three days, I knew I wasn't going to be released and to keep from succumbing to claustrophobia I sat on the edge of the makeshift bed and attempted to meditate. I had taken a class several years ago and concentrated on everything I could remember. The total silence and extreme darkness helped me focus and before long, I found myself having an out-of-body experience."

Many people turned to look at their neighbors and murmured in disbelief. Someone called out, "What happened then?"

Silence resumed as everyone awaited my answer. I twisted the corner of the sea fan tablecloth in trembling hands and glanced at Nathan for reassurance. His calm air and slight nod encouraged me to continue.

"I floated up near the ceiling, looking down at myself on the edge of the bed. I had heard about this type of thing so I thought I should be able to pass through the bars. I was right— I swam through them as though they weren't even there."

The murmur in the room began again, growing louder as more people realized what I had said. The whiskey-worms' influence became apparent when voices grew even shriller. Tinami's aide once again gained everyone's attention with the conch shell. When all was quiet, Tinami nodded.

"I swam outside and saw the beam of light. As I tried to figure out what it might be or what I should do next, a pod of dolphins appeared. One swam up to me and seemed to be urging me to come with her. I held onto her dorsal fin and she brought me back here to the cavern."

Before the new murmur could get very loud, I spoke over it and recaptured their attention. "I know this sounds preposterous, but that's what happened. I don't understand it any more than you do, but I'm just glad the dolphins were there." This time when I paused, everyone waited in silence.

"I swam directly to Dr. Nathan's room because he and I are friends and I knew he would help me, no matter how odd or implausible the story sounded. He gathered five of the strongest mermaids, asked them to bring bone pry bars, and the dolphins guided us back to the cell. My body was still sitting on the edge of the bed and I re-entered it. The mermaids found the weakest bar and pried it away from the wall and we came home."

This time, the murmur quickly swelled to a roar as questions were shouted. "Who did this?" "Who would want to hurt you?" "Can you talk to the dolphins? Did you call them to help you?" Some of the voices sounded scared, some belligerent.

Frightened, I looked at Nathan.

He glanced around at the increasingly hostile crowd. "We should leave." He motioned to Tinami and his aide darted to my side with instructions to lead me back to my room. Several other aides accompanied us to our cubicles to be sure no one followed and we could hear the commotion escalating as we hurried away.

Nathan and I sat and talked a while before he left and I finally broached the subject that was foremost in my mind. "Nathan, do you think they believed me? There were some questions we hadn't thought to address."

He pulled me close for a reassuring hug. "Relax, Serena. I was watching the faces as you talked and I think most believed you. Besides, everyone except us had too much alcohol and probably won't remember the details tomorrow, anyway." He kissed me goodnight.

Before leaving, though, he said, "I'm going to ask Tinami to post a guard outside your room until we can figure out what to do. I'm not taking a chance that someone can harm you."

I started to protest, then thought better of it. With love in his voice, Nathan said, "Please don't argue with me, Serena. I can't lose you."

I nodded and, still exhausted from my ordeal, barely heard him leave my cubicle. Sleep claimed me almost immediately, and, in spite of my recent fears and unusual experiences, no dreams or restlessness plagued me for the next eight hours. I awoke refreshed, feeling more positive about the future than I had for several weeks.

Nathan and I resumed our morning swims and afternoon seminars, dropping back into our usual routines. Kalani had suspected we hadn't told the whole story at dinner and we later filled her in on our suspicions about Valkar.

She agreed with our theory. "I think Valkar is certainly capable of such ruthlessness, especially if she believes you stand in the way of her getting what she wants. Please be careful, Serena. And let me know if I can help in any way."

And with so much attention focused in my direction, Maia and I agreed to wait a while before beginning our afternoon hunting and foraging sessions.

Life returned to normal and eventually Tinami decided the guard was unnecessary.

Feeling vulnerable, I couldn't relax completely. Knowing Valkar had masterminded my abduction, intending for me to die in that cell, kept the knots in my stomach from loosening their hold. On the surface, I seemed to be enjoying life and my friends; inside, I was a roiling mass of nerves. I knew Valkar would strike again, I just didn't know when or how. That uncertainty kept me in a constant state of vigilance.

One night, about two weeks later, I readied for bed, climbed under the covers, and tried to relax. Knowing no one guarded the entrance to my room, I tossed restlessly, sleeping in short stretches.

Suddenly, I awoke to a slight noise in the darkness and felt a ripple in the water. After the abduction, unexpected movement in the darkness could only be a threat, so I instinctively rolled away and flattened myself against the wall. I felt another, stronger ripple and a silken strand of cobwebs slipped across my face. Certain there was another presence in the room, I remained completely still. When I heard and felt nothing more for what seemed like hours, I gingerly climbed off the foot of the bed and shook a small box on the side table. It contained glow worms that emitted a greenish light when annoyed, giving off enough radiance that I could faintly see the room.

To my horror, a branch of coral protruded from the center of the bed, right where my heart would have been had I not rolled away. As I stared in disbelief, a long black strand floated up in the water and caught on the coral.

I gasped and recoiled, taking two quick steps back to the wall as though the hair was a poisonous snake set to strike. Propped against the rough stone wall, my body began to tremble, quaking as though the earth itself heaved beneath my feet. My breath came fast and shallow, my legs gave out, and I staggered to the foot of the bed. In shock, I sat staring at that long black hair, unable to think or act.

Finally, a sob escaped my throat and the small sound brought me back to life. I couldn't sit there and do nothing when my entire existence was being threatened. How would I be able to defend my husband and my child if a mere hair could shake me to the core? Determination and a steely resolve I didn't know I possessed rose to the surface. I would *not* let Valkar do this to me!

I arranged a pile of sand under the covers to resemble the shape of a sleeping body, allowed the worms to relax and stop glowing, and spent the rest of the night sitting in a corner, holding the piece of coral like a weapon. I would be prepared if Valkar returned—surprise and fortitude on my side.

Nothing more transpired for the next few hours and in the morning when I told Nathan about the attack, he had a visceral reaction to the threat on my life. "Valkar *must* be stopped! She can't physically attack you and get away with it."

He darted to my side and took me in his arms, hugging me tightly. "I can't lose you. I can't. What would I do..." Once again he choked. Without words, he buried his face in my hair.

I murmured softly. "Nathan, I'm alright. Please, look at me."

He raised his eyes to mine and I fell in love with those emerald orbs all over again. The intensity of his love held my gaze for a long moment and then he broke away, swimming rapidly toward the door. He growled, "I'm going to find Valkar."

"No! Nathan!" He stopped at the fear and underlying determination in my voice. "We can't confront her and make a scene. We need a plan. Please. Besides, the mermaids are out hunting and won't be back for hours."

He let out a deep breath and I could see him relax. "You're right. We do need a plan." He swam over and took me in his arms again, much more gently, and held me close. I felt the warmth of his cheek as he whispered in my ear. "What would I do without you?"

I melted against his warmth and held him tenderly, basking in his love. "And what would I do without *you*?"

After a long moment, we separated and began hashing over the situation again, the latest incident fueling our thoughts. No longer could we wait and see what Tinami and Saya might decide. We had to do something, before Valkar acted again.

After much debate, we decided to go to Tinami and Saya and tell them the truth, throwing ourselves on their mercy. We couldn't remain in the cavern, not with Valkar there, and could only hope the benevolent rulers would allow us to leave and give us enough time to prepare adequately for our departure.

Normally, anyone with an issue to discuss with the leaders would meet in the common room after lunch. Each problem would be dealt with on an individual basis and the rulers would take whatever time was needed to deal with it fairly. This day, no one else appeared. Nathan and I were shown in almost immediately.

We bowed our heads in respect and waited until Tinami spoke.

"Good afternoon, Nathan, Serena. What issue do you need to discuss today?"

Nathan began the story with the day we bumped into each other outside the common room and left little out up to the present, except for our physical relationship and the fact that he was pregnant. He also elaborated on our suspicions that Valkar was behind my abduction, apologizing for previously withholding this information.

The rulers listened without interrupting until Nathan explained about the previous night's attack. Tinami and Saya both leaned forward in their seats and directed the next question to me.

"What did you do to provoke such a serious attack?"

I shook my head. "Nothing. Valkar came to my room one day about a month ago and threatened me with physical harm if I didn't distance myself from Nathan. She said he belongs to her. Since then we've had no further interaction."

To my utter disbelief, Saya agreed with Valkar. "Nathan does belong to her. You have no claim to him and she has every right to protect her promised mate from an outsider, although the abduction and the physical attack are a bit drastic. If we were dealing with anyone but the sirene doctor, you would both have been banished months ago.

"We were hoping you'd come to your senses, Nathan, and honor your commitment to the sirene and your dead wife's sister. You know our law decrees you will marry Valkar."

Keeping his voice low and non-confrontational, Nathan replied, "Yes, Saya, our law is very clear. But you know Valkar is unstable and this latest attack proves it. When I came to the sirene as a young merkid, you took me in and raised me as your own. I have tried to be a good son; I've repaid you by becoming a doctor and helping our people. I've never expected preferential treatment but now I am asking for lenience and compassion."

He took one step toward Tinami and Saya and knelt on one knee. His voice wavered. "I love Serena the way you two love each other. I have seen first-hand the deep feelings you share and I've found that with her. I beg of you, please allow Serena and me to leave the sirene together."

He glanced at me and then back to the rulers. His voice remained low but became hard as he spoke of Valkar. "If you forbid me to leave and send Serena away, I will not marry Valkar. Our law is also very clear on this—you must put me to death for refusing to obey. Either way, I cannot stay."

I gasped at this revelation. I didn't know Nathan would be put to death for refusing to marry Valkar.

Tinami sighed as Nathan played his last and final card. "I know you must have a sirene doctor, but Kalani does an excellent job of caring for the health of our people. For the past several months, we've been studying together, sharing information for the betterment of our group. Kalani now knows many of the new methods of treatment to add to her old, traditional ways. She should be very effective."

When Nathan stopped speaking and lowered his head, Saya asked, "Do you have anything else to add? Serena?"

We shook our heads and were shown to the common room while Tinami and Saya pondered the situation and discussed it between them. Our futures, the future of our unborn child, and our very lives depended on their decision. And from what I'd heard so far, I wasn't optimistic. I truly thought I would be sent away to die alone…to lose the only man who had ever claimed my heart. And in the process, Nathan and our unborn child would also die.

As soon as the door closed behind us, leaving us alone in the common room, I whirled on Nathan. "Why didn't you tell me you'd be put to death for refusing to marry Valkar? If I'm sent away alone, you and our child will die, too, unless you marry her!"

"I knew if I told you, you'd insist I marry Valkar. The timing would be too far off to try and pass the child off as hers. And since the child will be half human, it might have two legs instead of a tail. Regardless, Valkar would *never* raise another woman's child."

I recognized the truth in what he said and couldn't see any other solution. Our fates were truly in Tinami and Saya's hands.

Nathan swam erratically back and forth across the room. I tried sitting, then standing, then pacing. *What was taking so long?*

A thought suddenly occurred to me and I stopped. Nathan bumped into me from behind. I startled him when I whirled and began babbling. "We can leave. We can leave now and swim as far and as fast as we can. Now! We have to go *now!*"

Before Nathan could even reply, the door opened and we were summoned for their judgment. My heart sank as we approached the rulers.

With a distinct chill in her voice, Saya first addressed me. "Serena, we welcomed you into our sirene when you were injured, doctored you, healed you, and befriended you. We fed you and gave you lodging, asking nothing in return. You have repaid us by disgracing our doctor, making a mockery of our laws, and causing dissension amongst our people. You will leave the cavern with nothing but what you brought with you."

With little hope left, I heard Tinami address Nathan. "You have been a valued member of this sirene since you were a young merkid and an honorable merman, until now. We took you in and treated you as a son. We have loved you and were proud that you became such a fine doctor. But your behavior now is disgraceful and a very poor example for the children who look up to you, as well as an embarrassment to us as rulers. If we did not have Kalani to doctor our people, you would stay and deal with the unpleasant consequences. However, since you are family, we have decided to do the only thing we can do without enforcing the strictest of our laws and, ultimately, putting you to death. We will elevate Kalani to the status of sirene doctor, effective immediately. You no longer have any rights of citizenship in our group."

Looking back and forth between us, Tinami said, "You have two days to leave the cavern, taking only what food you can carry." His voice took on a hard edge and his eyes narrowed to dangerous slits. "If you survive, you will make a nest far enough from here that you will never cross paths with our hunting parties. If they meet either of you while foraging, they will take your life and bring me your head. Go."

His words sent chills up my spine.

We were summarily dismissed and escorted to the door.

Nathan and I started to swim back to my cubicle. Once out of sight, I turned to him with a stricken look. I frantically whispered, "I'm so scared! What if Valkar hears about the decree and comes to my room tonight? This time she'll make sure she kills me. If I'm no longer in the picture, she'll believe you can stay and marry her and she'll have what she wants. And once she finds out you're having our child, she'll kill the baby and probably you, too. She won't tolerate being humiliated."

"You're right. We can't risk Valkar's jealousy and mental instability any longer. Even though it's not the best of plans, we need to visit Kalani to say goodbye. We'll ask her to prepare us some food and we'll leave tonight."

I wanted to see Maia and Kiki again, to thank them for saving my life and being my friends, but knew we had to move quickly. I wished I had asked Maia earlier to teach me to hunt; now it was too late. With heavy hearts, we swam to Kalani's lab.

One look at our sad faces told her we brought bad news. "Tinami and Saya agreed we can leave but we only have two days. And if Valkar hears about the decree, she won't waste any time in coming after Serena again. So we need to leave now. Tonight."

"*Tonight?*" Kalani was obviously shocked that we wanted to leave immediately. "You should make a list of everything you need—you don't want to be far away and find you forgot something important. You need food, supplies, weapons. How can you leave tonight?"

"Kalani, Serena's life is at risk if we stay. Valkar won't take a chance on letting me leave, believing if Serena is dead I'll stay and marry her. She was always jealous of Saralee's status as the doctor's wife and she won't let the opportunity pass to gain that position for herself. Now that we have permission to leave together, we have to go *now*."

Finally realizing we weren't running off without giving it serious thought, Kalani agreed it was for the best. She didn't like it, but knew we had to go. "I'll make some wraps and snacks. I'm always in the kitchen at odd hours so no one will be suspicious if they see me puttering around in there. Wait here."

When Kalani returned, she gave us enough food for several days and snacks to help sustain us on our journey. When Nathan took the package, Kalani also handed him a wickedly sharp bone knife. "Please, take this, too. I hope you never need it."

We had no idea where we were going and knew we'd never see our dear friend again. All three of us sobbed openly as we hugged goodbye. She showed us to her private entrance and Nathan and I swam away.

Feeling as though my heart was breaking, yet knowing we were doing the right thing for our growing family, I followed Nathan out of the cavern.

With only three hours before sunset, we swam quickly, knowing we had to be well away before the morning hunt began. I recognized many of the coral heads, cave openings, and rock formations that Nathan and I had passed on our daily swims, including our place. The little cave where we'd made love so many times would soon be only a lovely memory.

Eventually, we entered new territory and I could tell from Nathan's body language that he was on high alert. We swam, hand-in-hand, until exhaustion forced us to stop. We spied a small opening nearby and Nathan told me to wait until he looked inside.

When he returned and assured me the cave was uninhabited, we entered together. Settling near the back with some rocks for a rough table, we opened the package of food Kalani had sent. We smiled as we thought of our friend and saw the abundance she had prepared. Wraps made of kelp and other underwater greens; sushi, oysters, crab cakes, lobster, and chunks of fish; and shrimp salad. In a separate package we found fruit, snacks, and desserts; kelp chips, lobster squares, and a fruity, sweet dessert salad. We quickly devoured a couple of the wraps and curled up in the back corner. Immediately, we fell into a deep sleep brought on by physical and emotional exhaustion.

In the morning, anxious to be on our way, we decided to swim for a while before eating. Tinami's dire warning haunted our thoughts. "If they meet either of you while foraging, they will take your life and bring me your head." We swam away from our night's lodging, purpose and determination goading us into a quick pace.

Finally, about noon, we slowed and looked for a small cave where we could relax and eat our brunch. "There!" I was proud to have spotted the fissure before Nathan, wanting to take a more active role in support of my family. I insisted on performing the preliminary safety check while Nathan waited impatiently outside. When I tugged him into the doorway, he hugged me tightly. Seated on the floor, we enjoyed a meal of sushi, salad, and fruit, rested, and left the cozy little space to swim some more.

We repeated the pattern for another day and finished off the last of the food that Kalani had given us about noon. Totally drained by that evening and in need of sleep, we took refuge in another small cave. Nathan held me in his arms as we talked about where we should build our nest. A small seed of hope finally began to sprout in my heart and we fell asleep, nuzzling each other and giggling into the darkness. We finally felt safe.

At dawn I awoke, hungry and anxious to start looking for our new home. Nathan surprised me by rolling me onto my back and looking deep into my eyes. He was so still and looked so somber, I was afraid something was amiss.

"What? Why are you so serious? Is something wrong? Is the baby okay?" I babbled questions at him so quickly he didn't have time to answer.

"I'm fine. The baby's fine. I just need to hear you say you're *really* okay with this. That you want to make a life with me and begin our own sirene. I need to hear you say you love me."

"Oh, Nathan," I breathed. "I've never loved someone so much in all my life. I'm so much *more* than okay with this—I want this with every cell in my body. All I want is to be with you, with our child, to make a life with our little family. I've waited forever for you to come into my life and I'm *never* going to let you go."

My eyes burned with tears as he kissed me, long and slow and deep. I could feel his heart beating in sync with mine and my hand slipped to his belly where our baby moved contentedly inside him. It was the first time I'd felt it move and the feeling startled me. I pulled back, surprised, and we placed our hands together on his abdomen. At that moment, there was no sirene, no Valkar, no threats on our lives—only love, commitment to each other, and a mutual determination to make a home where our child could grow up safely.

We looked around at our temporary haven, sighed, and reluctantly separated, knowing we'd better start house hunting. This was a nice area, full of healthy coral, sponges, sea fans, and a drop-off a short distance away—and it was far enough from Tinami and Saya's cavern. It allowed access to deeper water as well as a shallower, sandy-bottomed stretch perfect for a youngster to play in. All we needed was to locate a nice-sized cavern or nearby cave system where we could establish our new home.

An hour later, Nathan pointed to a small fissure barely visible from where we drifted above the sea bottom. Curious to see if it opened into a cave, we swam down to investigate. True to form, Nathan wanted me to wait at the entrance while he looked inside, but I insisted on going it alone. After only a moment, I excitedly grabbed his hand and pulled him inside. It was perfect!

The small cave in the front acted as a protective foyer that led into a larger cavern. To the right, another small cave provided additional living space. It offered enough room for a small family but was secure enough that nothing too large could swim in and surprise us. And from the front opening, we had a great view that overlooked the sandy stretch with the deeper blue beyond. I couldn't have imagined anything more ideal.

We happily explored the space and discovered a small opening at the rear of the main cavern. Not knowing what might be lurking, Nathan wanted to check it out as he usually did.

I surprised him by refusing to take a passive position. "I need to assume more of the mermaid's role, Nathan. Let me do this."

He acquiesced, looking a bit pleased at my assertiveness. But before I could swim into the opening, he pulled Kalani's knife out of the pack and handed it to me. "Just in case."

I nodded and gripped the handle firmly.

Not knowing where the tight tunnel might lead or what could be hiding in the darkness, I slowly finned through the passageway, holding the knife in front of me. As I approached each bend, I paused and took a deep breath to steady my nerves and before long, I swam out a small opening at the rear of our new home. I returned to find Nathan impatiently swimming to and fro.

"It leads outside, away from the drop-off. It's the perfect escape route should anything happen in here that blocks the main entryway. This place was made for us!"

He took me in his arms. "I'm so proud of you! You're a mermaid at heart." We giggled and surveyed our new home.

The location was three full days' swim from our old cavern. We knew Tinami's hunting parties foraged, at most, four to six hours' distant from the main cavern. We felt safe in our new neighborhood and found that it offered much snack food right outside the front door. Nathan pointed out areas that would be perfect homes for crabs, shrimp, and small fish.

We began cleaning out debris and old shells and coral, making our new home as comfortable as we could at the moment. Rocks formed the frame for a bed—until we could locate a large clam shell—and we brought in sand and bundles of kelp to make it softer. Additional rocks and large shells created makeshift tables and chairs. As with any new home, the projects were endless.

CHAPTER 10

OUR DAILY LIVES fell into a comfortable routine. Home took on a cozy and relaxed atmosphere and Nathan taught me as best he could about foraging and hunting for food. It would take time, but I knew my skills would improve and there was such abundance just outside our door that we would never go hungry.

In the beginning, we ate a lot of clams, oysters, and other sea life that didn't use speed or agility to evade predators. I learned which grasses, kelp, and underwater plants were edible and tasty and I determined to practice catching lobster and small fish so our diet could be varied and healthy. Eventually, I would become proficient at hunting squid, octopus, and larger fish, as well.

During quiet times, Nathan showed me how to fashion a spear from bone or, occasionally, a long branch of coral. Bone was stronger and more durable, best for hunting larger game.

The baby in Nathan's belly grew and he became awkward in the water, tiring easily. The fetus had slipped from the sac into his pouch and would be born in less than a month. We often relaxed after lunch, our bodies curled together, and talked about the baby, boy-versus-girl names, and what life would be like once we were three.

One morning, we headed to our favorite spot to bag some lobster. We'd been there before and knew they grew big and juicy in this location, but it was quite a distance from home. Although it was a long swim, it was the only way to satisfy Nathan's pregnancy craving. We swam slowly, stopping at intervals to let him rest his unwieldy body. I became concerned when it was obvious the rest stops weren't helping.

Finally, Nathan told me to go on without him; he was going to head back and take a nap. His time was near and I knew he must be extremely uncomfortable since he *never* sent me out alone.

I offered to swim back with him but he waved me off. "Don't be ridiculous. I'll be fine. You be careful—don't let those huge lobsters haul you away!"

In addition, I wondered if I'd be able to catch enough lobster on my own to make a satisfactory meal—normally, we worked as a team.

He gave me the knife that had become our "safety talisman," we laughed, and he kissed me. I ran my hand lovingly over his belly and smiled into those captivating green eyes.

Our life was perfect. I had never been happier and certainly never more in love. This wonderful merman was my rock, my world, and I couldn't wait to begin our life as parents. My heart was bursting with joy and I reluctantly stayed behind as my beloved swam awkwardly toward home.

Beneath the joy, I had a niggling feeling that something wasn't quite right but didn't want to make Nathan feel helpless and vulnerable by insisting on going with him. I turned and started toward the lobster field. The farther I went, the stronger that horrible feeling of impending doom became.

Finally, I couldn't stand it any longer. I whirled and bolted for home. Racing as fast as I could, I scanned the water for some sign of Nathan. Nothing.

I rounded a rocky outcropping and there! There he was, resting against a large rock, his head hanging down, eyes closed. I gulped a huge sigh of relief, knowing he was alright. I felt silly. All that impending doom stuff seemed ridiculous and I smiled to myself. I waited behind the rocks for a few moments to catch my breath, keeping out of sight so as not to embarrass Nathan should he look up and see me.

I peeked out from the rocks as I was about to turn back to The Great Lobster Hunt.

And that's when I saw it.

A huge tiger shark glided up over the edge of the wall like a sleek and dangerous shadow. I tried to recall what Nathan had told me about shark behavior and my heart began to race. Frozen in place, I couldn't move…couldn't help.

The shark swam lazily in Nathan's general direction and I tried to convince myself it hadn't seen him. Then there was a subtle change in the shark's movements. It swam faster… A bit more erratically… It hunched its back. Lowered its pectoral fins. Then it made a tight turn to the right. I almost sighed in audible relief as it swam away from where Nathan rested.

I saw him push off from the big boulder and strike out for home. Oblivious to the danger, he swam with determined flicks of his tail, moving farther and farther from the scant protection of the rock.

Suddenly the shark banked sharply. I watched in horror as it sped directly at Nathan. Its speed increased as it focused on its unsuspecting prey.

Nathan never saw the shark that killed him. Hit from behind, he was nearly torn in two. The contraction of his dying body expelled our unborn child too early into a dangerous world.

The predator fed voraciously, greedily devouring flesh and gore from the now-murky water. Thankfully, I was unable to clearly see what happened. Then I spotted the still-struggling fetus as it drifted slowly toward the sea floor.

"My baby!" Without fear for myself, I darted forward, knife in hand. Maternal instinct screamed at me to protect my child. Then I braked as the shadowy torpedo zoomed downward and swallowed him in a single bite.

I snapped. With a visceral need to get my hands on the murderous shark, I bolted toward the scene of the carnage. My mouth opened wide in a primal scream. "NOOOOOO

CHAPTER 11

"NOOOOOO...!"

I screwed my eyes shut to wipe out the horrific scene, my heart shattered, my life over. I *wanted* the shark to attack me. As he ended my life, I would spill his blood as well. I had nothing left to live for.

As I opened my eyes, red water, carnage, and death had been replaced by white tiled walls and a strong antiseptic smell.

"What the...? Where...? How did I...?" Confusion merged with the terror in my soul and panic washed over me like a rogue wave.

Doctors and nurses flocked to my bedside drawn, undoubtedly, by the scream that had left my throat raw. I heard voices, a PA system paging Dr. Hollister, and a nurse at my side talking about a scuba diving accident.

I felt the bed move beneath me as someone came close, too close. I had to get away! I clawed at the bed covers. Threw them back and ripped a tube out of my arm. Warm red blood stained stark white sheets. Perplexed, I saw blood spreading on both sheets and in the water.

Through the fog in my mind I heard a nurse address the doctor at my bedside. "I've never seen you become so personally involved in a patient before, but all that extra time and attention has paid off."

"No patient has ever affected me like she did," a deeper voice said. "I couldn't give up on her." He stepped closer.

Strong arms wrapped around me from behind as a nurse moved tubes and monitors away from the bed. I struggled and kicked and screamed in senseless panic. Then…a voice. A soft, sweet voice I knew so well whispered in my ear. "You're safe. Shhhhh…. Relax, I've got you. I'll save you. Nothing can hurt you. I promise."

It was *his* voice, Nathan's voice! But I saw the shark… It *was* his voice, though—I knew it in my soul. I stopped struggling and turned my head. I saw his face, his beautiful, amazing, wonderful face. Nathan!

I desperately clutched his warm hands. As I stared, my shattered heart stumbled and resumed its normal beat. His voice and reassuring smile were tender and comforting. I felt safe—leaning on the steady rock in my life. I studied his magnificent green eyes framed with dark lashes, the silver hair with just a hint of curl, the strong, square jaw with the deep cleft in his chin. The best-looking man I'd ever laid eyes on.

Terror receded as I realized I was not underwater, was not faced with the unspeakable death of my husband and unborn child, was not bereft and alone in an alien world. I smiled tentatively through the tears, noting the loving expression on Dr. Nathan's face and the warm emotion in his eyes. The trembling in my body eased as I recalled my coma-Nathan's arms around me, his loving touch, and our deep commitment to one another. Good memories of our life together slowly overtook the horror of the last few minutes and I felt profound gratitude for being given a second chance to drown in those magnificent green eyes.

CHAPTER 12

Seven years later...

AFTER I RECOVERED from the concussion, broken arm, near-drowning, and coma following the boating accident, Dr. Nathan Hollister and I developed a real-life relationship. I remembered every minute of the time I'd spent underwater with my mermaid friends: Maia, Kalani, Kiki, and of course, Nathan, as well as Tinami, Saya, and the ruthless Valkar. I missed them and wondered how they were...if they thought of me.

But I tried not to dwell on it, instead choosing to live my life in the present realm. My feelings for Dr. Nathan were inevitably an extension of my deep love for the merman Nathan, but there was no way to separate them. And as I discovered, the human Nathan was every bit as loving, kind, and chivalrous as the other.

We married within six months of my leaving the hospital and found ourselves with child soon thereafter—me, not him. This pregnancy was bittersweet, bringing back memories of the horrific loss of our first child. But the happy far outweighed the sad and we soon found ourselves the parents of a healthy, bouncing baby boy.

We named him Dylan, from the Welsh language meaning "son of the sea." It seemed appropriate. And he loved anything to do with being on, in, or around the water—fishing, swimming, boating, or just hanging around the dock.

Nathan had owned a boat when we married and we upgraded to a larger, more family-friendly craft after Dylan was born. We often went diving and snorkeling or simply enjoyed a relaxing day of waves and ocean breezes. "Boat" was one of Dylan's very first words and from the time he learned to walk, he loved the *Serena* more than anything.

As he grew older and his friends wanted to play sports or video games, Dylan preferred boating and fishing, so we spent a lot of time as a family on and in the water.

Nathan and I hadn't told Dylan about my boating accident or my underwater coma experience, but one day while we were enjoying a balmy day on the *Serena*, I broached the subject.

"Dylan, do you know what mermaids are?" I had no idea what kind of answer to expect, but his reply shocked me.

"Of course, Mom, everybody knows about mermaids—they're part women and part fish. Why?"

"Well, back before I met your dad, I had a boating accident and almost died."

Intrigued, Dylan turned an earnest face my direction. "Really? What happened? And what's that got to do with mermaids?"

I explained how I'd leapt back into the water to swim with dolphins forgetting that I still had my dive weights strapped around my waist. He was so engrossed in the story that I told him the entire tale up to where merman-Nathan and I had gone lobster hunting. I paused, unsure how much I should say.

"Is that when he was killed by the shark, Mom?"

I froze, suddenly cold in the afternoon sunlight. "What shark, Dylan?"

"You know, the shark that killed Nathan and your baby. He would've been my brother, right?"

More sharply than I intended, I asked, "Who told you about the shark? And the baby?"

"Nobody." He shrugged dismissively as only six-year-old boys can. "I just know." His innocence and certainty on the subject confused the hell out of me. *How could he know this?*

Just then Nathan came up from the galley with iced tea and cookies. "How about a snack for my favorite family?"

Dylan giggled. "Daaa-aad, we're your *only* family!"

"That's right," Nathan said, "and that's the way I like it." He tickled Dylan with one hand and placed the tray of cookies and tea in front of us. Then he noticed how pale I was under my tan.

"Are you okay, Honey? You look kind of grey." He frowned and reached over to place the back of his hand on my forehead.

"She told me how she almost died and went to live with the mermaids!"

"She did?" He looked at me questioningly. One eyebrow rose inquisitively as it always did when he didn't understand something.

"Yeah, but I already knew about the mermaids and stuff. And the shark that killed Nathan and her baby. I don't think I want a brother. I like our family just the way it is. Can I have another cookie?"

"Sure you can." Puzzled, Nathan eyed me again. The raised eyebrow had been replaced by a deep vee creasing his forehead. "You told him that?"

"No. I didn't. He said he 'just knows.'"

I watched my innocent young son munching cookies in the late afternoon sunshine and felt gooseflesh roughen the skin on my arms. How could he know things he couldn't know?

"What do you mean 'he just knows'?" Nathan seemed as confused as I was.

"That's what he said. Then you came up with tea and cookies. I don't know any more than that."

"Okay." He turned toward Dylan. "Son, how do you know about the shark and the baby? Did someone tell you?"

"No." Another bite of cookie. "I have dreams."

"You do? What kind of dreams?"

"Mostly they're about mermaids and breathing underwater and stuff. That's why I wasn't surprised when Mom told me she'd lived with them. I want to live with them, too."

My husband and I exchanged surprised looks. Then he said, "Dylan, you do know that mermaids aren't real and people can't really live with them, don't you?"

Dylan put his iced tea down. "You've told me not to lie, so why are you lying to me?"

"We're not lying to you, son."

"Mom lived with the mermaids. That means they're real. If they're not real, then you lied to me!" His voice rose and his face flushed red—with anger or embarrassment, I wasn't sure.

Angry, he yelled, "They're real! I know they are! I've seen them and talked to them in my dreams. Stop lying!" He stormed away and stomped down the stairs to the galley.

Nathan and I sat in silence trying to understand what was happening. How had this beautiful afternoon turned into such an awful drama?

"Honey, I need to ask you something. It's bothered me for a while and now I think we should address it head on."

"What?"

"Do you really think you lived with the mermaids?"

"I… Well…" I looked down at my hands and sighed. "I don't know, Nathan. What I experienced after the accident was so real…"

"Honey, you *know* mermaids are just a myth."

"Do I? They saved my life! I would've died if not for Maia and Kiki. I've *tried* to put it behind me and believe it was only my subconscious keeping me alive long enough for my body to heal. But, Nathan, it's as real to me as this boat under my feet, as real as you and our son. How can I deny what I know in my heart is true?" Tears welled in my eyes and I looked away, then back to my husband.

"I fell in love with you while I was in that coma. You were there, underwater, taking care of me, healing me, protecting me, loving me. I thank God *every day* for that concussion because if it hadn't happened, we never would've met. Don't ask me not to believe!"

He hung his head and I ran to the bow. I'd cut off my right arm rather than hurt him but I was caught in a conundrum that seemed to have no solution. Asking me to deny the mer-people's existence was tantamount to asking me not to believe in him, in us, in our love. *How could I?*

I sobbed and wrestled with the dilemma until I felt his arms wrap around me from behind, just like he did that day in the hospital. That day coma-Nathan and our child were killed by the shark. My two realities were so intertwined that I couldn't tell where one ended and the other began.

He held me. Eventually the tears stopped and I gazed into his beloved face, into those bottomless emerald pools.

Looking past Nathan, I saw Dylan come up from below deck with something awkwardly wrapped around his waist.

Curious, I watched him. He walked to the stern and looked down into the water, then raised his face to me. Squinting in the bright sunlight, he smiled and waved. "I'm going to find the mermaids, Mommy!"

At that moment I realized he had strapped a weight belt around his middle. As I stood and screamed, "NOOOOO!" my son leapt into the ocean and sank rapidly out of sight.

Nathan dove headfirst off the bow. I ran below deck for the other weight belt—I knew I had to be able to sink far below where I could go without it. I would save my son or die trying.

I grabbed the belt and hurriedly buckled it on. Clutching my fins I dove off the stern. Sinking rapidly, I turned in the water and bent at the waist until I descended backside first. In this vee position, I was able to put my fins on while not slowing my descent.

Then I turned to face the bottom, kicking furiously. Dylan would go down very quickly because the weight belt was much heavier than his body required—I needed to catch up.

Already my lungs were screaming for air and I prayed for help. *Please don't let my son die. Please…*

Then I thought of the dolphin that had rescued me during my out-of-body experience. She had said I could call on her any time using the power of my mind. Continuing to kick, I closed my eyes and pictured Dylan. I called to the dolphin, begging for her help with my son.

And when I opened my eyes, there she was, swimming at my side, her thoughts touching my mind. "I'm here, Serena. We'll find him."

I grasped her dorsal fin and we torpedoed toward the bottom. Ahead, I discerned movement, but the force of the water against my eyes blurred my vision.

Suddenly, my lungs no longer labored, lack of air was not an issue, and I felt the familiar relaxation I had become so accustomed to when living with the mer-people. They were near.

A coral wall rose on my left; deep blue water stretched as far as I could see to the right. Far below, the sand sloped into the abyss.

Maia and Kiki materialized alongside us and the rest of Tinami and Saya's sirene fanned out in all directions. Maia swam beside the dolphin and I while I briefly explained.

"My son, it's my son, Maia! He's wearing a weight belt and will descend rapidly. We have to find him."

She darted away and the next thing I knew, the mer-people were combing the depths like a well-organized militia. They would find him. I could only pray it would be in time.

A deep, rhythmic thudding, amplified by the water, began in the distance, soon reverberating all around me—I felt it in my bones. *What is it?*

The dolphin stopped so suddenly I nearly catapulted over her head. "They've found him. He's okay. The drum is a signal." I heard the message in my mind and the warmth and sincere joy conveyed in those words moved me nearly to tears. I threw my arms around my dolphin friend and sagged against her, weak with relief.

"Where? Where is he?" I ached to hold Dylan in my arms, to see with my own eyes that he was alright.

"There." The dolphin bobbed her head toward the deepest blue water and as I stared, a throng of indistinct mer-people appeared, becoming clearer as they approached. Two lovely young mermaids held Dylan's hands, propelling him between them. His face radiated absolute delight and I could hear his constant giggles drifting through the water. My heart constricted with an almost palpable pain as I thought how close I'd come to losing him—and just how much I owed this group of mer-people and the dolphin.

"Mommy, Mommy, look! Mermaids! I told you I'd find them."

The two young mermaids swam up to me, smiled, and released Dylan's hands. He flung his arms around me in a hug so tight I could barely breathe—but I'm sure he felt the same in my embrace. I swore to myself I'd never let him go, but too soon he wriggled out of my grasp. "C'mon, Mom, let's check it out. This is the coolest place *ever*!"

Maia floated over and hugged me as he darted off with a couple young merkids. "He's beautiful, Serena. You and Nathan make great babies. Is he here?" She glanced around as though expecting him to appear.

"Oh, Maia, I've thought of you so often over the years. You wouldn't believe what has happened. I wish we could stay and visit with you and catch up on everything, but Nathan's waiting on the boat and I don't want him to think he's lost us both."

Her mystified expression prompted a few more details. "Merman-Nathan was killed by a shark—our unborn baby, too."

At her horrified look I rushed the next sentence. "But my human Nathan is just as wonderful—they're the same, Maia, and we can live together as a family above the surface. We have a wonderful life there, but I miss you and my mermaid friends. Is Kalani here? I'd love to see her."

Maia shook her head. "No, Kalani couldn't come. She has become frailer and is looking after some of the youngest merkids while all of the juveniles and adults are out here. Had she known it was *you*, I'm sure she would've insisted on joining the search party, though."

"Give her my love, okay? Tell her the food she sent with Nathan and I was perfect and just what we needed.

"Now, I need to corral my kid and get back to my husband. Will Dylan have any problem returning to the surface without mermaids nearby?"

A sudden deep voice stopped me cold. With affection in his tone, Tinami said, "Serena, I see you survived being expelled from the sirene. You look well."

I turned to face him, not sure what to expect. Surely, after all this time he posed no threat? "Yes, Tinami, I'm fine, thank you. Is Saya with you?"

"No, it is wise for one ruler to remain in the cavern. We heard your distress call and wanted to help." He must've noted the apprehension on my face. "You have nothing to fear from me, Serena, I wish you and your family well. Too much time has passed to cling to old transgressions."

"Thank you, Tinami." I sighed deeply, relieved. "I loved the time I spent in the sirene and think of my old life often. I'm glad to see the group doing well. However, I must go." Looking around, I added, "Where'd Dylan get off to now?"

As though she'd heard my question, the dolphin swam up with Dylan on her back. He was still smiling.

"It's time to go. Say goodbye to your new friends."

"Ah, Mom, can't we stay a little longer?"

"No, we can't. Your father must be worried sick. We've been gone quite a while. Now, say goodbye."

Maia, Kiki, and the two young mermaids who had been playing with Dylan offered to accompany us to the surface, darting questioning glances at Tinami.

Shocked, I turned to the ruler. "I thought mermaids were forbidden to go to the surface."

"They are, Serena. But you are nearly family and need our help. It would be much safer for a large group to ascend than just you and your son. I cannot, in good conscience, send you off alone. Come."

Many other mer-people joined us and we began the ascent, taking our time, look-outs at the edge of the group watching for threats along the way, and dolphins scouting ahead. When I spotted the bottom of the boat, my spirit soared, knowing Nathan would be waiting.

As we broke the surface, I saw my beloved sitting at the bow, his head hung in sadness, his entire body signaling loss, hopelessness, and despair. I ached, knowing our lengthy absence had caused him pain.

"Dad! Dad! Look! I found the mermaids!"

At the first word, Nathan's head whipped up and he stood. Then, shock and disbelief on his face, he stared down at the water teeming with dolphins and mermaids, his wife and son in the center of the melee.

"What the...?"

I waved. "We're fine, Nathan! Come meet my friends."

Without hesitation he leaped off the bow and stroked to my side. Gathering Dylan and I into a trembling embrace, he sobbed into my shoulder.

"We're okay, Honey, we're okay."

When the torrent subsided, I said, "I want to introduce you to my friends. They've saved my life twice and the life of our son. We owe them forever."

Fighting overwhelming emotion, he shook hands with every single member of the sirene. When I introduced Maia, he pulled her into a hug.

"I've heard so much about you and what you did for my wife…and now you've also saved my son. I can never thank you enough."

"Serena was a good friend when she lived with us. I am happy to help bring her and your son back to you. I feel like I know you, too, Nathan. Be well."

Nathan and Tinami shook hands and in a trembling voice, Nathan said, "Thanks to you and your people I have my family back. I don't know what I would've done without them. If there's ever anything I can do for you, please get word to us somehow."

"It has been over a hundred years since a human lived with a sirene, but Serena was a welcome addition until you took her away from us. The two of you will live on in our lore for many generations to come.

"Now, we must go."

We climbed into the stern and waved as one by one, they disappeared into the depths.

In my mind, I said goodbye to the dolphin who had so quickly answered my desperate call for help.

"Goodbye, Serena. Be happy!"

Nathan took me in his arms, kissed me tenderly, and whispered, "Okay, you proved your point—I'll never doubt you again."

I smiled mischievously. "Good to know. But now that our 'son of the sea' has met the mermaids, how are we going to keep him from wearing a weight belt every time he jumps into the ocean?"

AUTHOR'S NOTE

THANK YOU FOR taking the time to read "Saving Serena." For writers, there are few things more satisfying than knowing someone has enjoyed the words we put on paper.

I'm going to ask you to take another moment and leave a review at your favorite retailer – they are crucial to the success of the book.

Send me an email at bev@bevscherberger.com and I'll add you to my email list for future book notifications.

If you enjoyed "Saving Serena," you should like my full-length novel that also begins with a scuba diving mishap. It is available both as an e-book and in paperback form. You can read the first two chapters of "STRANDED" here.

STRANDED

SAMPLE CHAPTER 1

Lissy

MY DIVE BUDDY AND I finned head-first toward the bottom of the sea. I had visited Cozumel, Mexico, several times before and thoroughly enjoyed the drift dives common in this area. We didn't have to monitor the current, navigate back to the boat, or watch for an exit point. Jumping into the water and drifting with the flow allowed us to simply "be" and relax into the whole dive experience.

I knew the captain would observe our bubbles and follow along in the current, ready to motor over and pick us up when we surfaced. He would also be alert and nearby in case of an emergency. It couldn't get any easier.

Of course, I'd heard horror stories of people being left behind following a drift dive, but couldn't imagine how that could easily happen. If there were fourteen divers to begin with the captain just had to count bodies before heading back to shore. Certain that our captain and crew were competent enough to ensure that everyone was present and accounted for, I turned my attention to my new dive partner.

We had met the previous day. Following the morning dives, our group had mingled with the locals at a popular lunch bar. With plenty of tequila and tacos for everyone, we'd made new Mexican friends. We were on vacation! It was the perfect time to let loose.

Across the bar, I noticed a tall, attractive guy staring in my direction. Before making a fool of myself, I turned to my right and glanced around to be sure he wasn't making eyes at someone behind me. *Nope, nobody looking his way.* When I turned back, prepared to practice my rusty flirting skills, there was only an empty space at the bar. Not even a beer bottle to indicate he might return. *Hmpf… Missed my chance.*

A smooth voice, speaking English with a strong Mexican accent, startled me out of my pout. "Hola. You dive weeth these Americanos, no?" I raised my head to see the vision from across the bar standing at my side. Up close, he was even better-looking than I'd thought. A shock of wavy black hair fell into his eyes and as he brushed it back, I appreciated the careless look emphasized by his well-worn T-shirt and snug-fitting jeans. Soft curls brushed his shoulders and he gave his head a sexy toss to throw it off his face. Broad shoulders, olive skin, a square, masculine jaw, and perfect white teeth completed the package. His intimate smile, coupled with intense dark eyes that bored into mine, made me blush. He stood so close his left leg brushed the naked skin of my thigh. I wished I hadn't worn shorts.

"Yes, I'm with the group." Anxious to keep the conversation going, I asked, "Are you? A diver?"

"Sí, I dive weeth mi padre for many years, then mis amigos. I know many very good places to go. Places not for tourists. You would go there weeth me?" I looked up into his bottomless dark eyes and found myself unwilling to say no. But I couldn't just go off with a total stranger. My mind searched frantically for an acceptable way to spend time with this Latin hunk.

I had an idea. "Why don't you dive with our group tomorrow? Maybe the captain would let you select the site and you can show us some of your favorite spots." I smiled back, hoping he'd say yes.

"What ees your boat?" When I told him the name of the dive operation and that our captain's name was Carlos, he nodded. "Sí, es mi amigo. I speak to heem and arrange for special dive weeth your group tomorrow. You weel like thees beauteeful place."

Putting his empty bottle on the bar, he said, "I am Rodrigo. You call me Rigo. And what are you called, beauteeful American chica?"

Again, I blushed. "My name is Alyssa, but my friends call me Lissy."

"I like Leesa more better. That I weel call you. Hasta mañana, Leesa!" I could feel the heat in my face as he walked away, the tight jeans hugging the curve of his ass.

"Oh, my God, Lissy! Who was *that*?" Two of the girls from the dive group descended on me with a barrage of questions.

"How did you meet him?" "What's his name?" "Does he have any gorgeous friends?" I explained that he was going to talk to Captain Carlos and see if he could dive with us in the morning. I was hoping to see the beautiful places Rigo had told me about, not to mention the beautiful Rigo himself.

And sure enough, the next morning, he was on the dock talking animatedly with Captain Carlos. The two men pointed seaward and nodded, evidently in agreement. The butterflies in my stomach threatened to come right up my throat as Rigo glanced in my direction and smiled. I nearly melted into a puddle there on the dock, but my friend Joanne grabbed my elbow and kept us both moving.

"Hola, Leesa! Buenos días! We weel dive on a beauteeful place. You weel theenk eet ees perfect." In true Latin fashion, he kissed me on both cheeks, causing my face to flush again. I introduced him to Joanne and he charmed her immediately. "You weel be Cho, pretty amiga of Leesa."

The crew efficiently loaded the scuba tanks onto the boat. Our fourteen divers arrived in various small clusters and eagerly boarded, stowing personal gear under the bench seats. As the boat motored slowly away from the dock, I introduced Rigo to my friends and told them about the non-touristy dive site.

Captain Carlos came up on deck and asked for our attention. "Good morning, divers! Today, thanks to Rigo, you will dive on a very beautiful reef. It's much more secluded and farther away than we usually go – almost two hours – so get comfortable. It's not visited by the dive operations in Cozumel because of the distance so it's pristine." We all grinned and applauded our new friend. "Yay, Rigo!" "We'll buy you all the beer you can drink tonight!"

The captain continued. "You'll have to watch your depth in this location. The bottom slopes to a drop-off that is way too deep for sport diving – over three hundred feet – and the current can be tricky. Try not to get separated from the group. You might see whales or sharks so be sure to take your cameras." We cheered, thrilled about a new adventure.

Everyone chatted enthusiastically for the first hour. Later, lulled by the heat of the sun and the drone of the boat's motor, some napped. At last, Captain Carlos cut the engine and Rigo announced, "We are here! The perfect place for to dive!" We cheered and began donning our gear. When everyone was ready, the captain motioned for us to enter the water. "Please, be careful, watch your depth, and when you surface, I'll come pick you up."

Although I'd noticed a storm brewing in the distance and the dark clouds on the horizon had become even more ominous during the lengthy ride, the sun shone brightly on us as we rolled backwards off the boat. All was calm and serene underwater.

As Rigo and I cruised downward, we saw the others descending around us. The group leveled off above the bottom at a depth of sixty feet and it quickly became apparent that Captain Carlos was right about the tricky current. We zoomed along, alert for humongous rocks jutting up from the sea floor. Many were as large as small houses, but thankfully, the visibility was good so we could avoid them by angling left or right. At this depth, the water filtered out color, leaving the scene various shades of blue-grey. Darker shadows hid entrances to caverns and swim-through arches created by overlapping rocks. Boulders of all sizes and shapes dotted the floor; stands of spiky Elkhorn Coral decorated the areas in between. As we zoomed over the seascape, the rocky floor gave way to a coral reef punctuated by massive rock formations.

The reef was, indeed, pristine and beautiful. I saw no broken coral or dead white branches. Everything was healthy with a wide variety of marine life. Many different types of sponges and coral provided homes for a plethora of fish, but we were moving so quickly it was impossible to take photos. Afraid of slamming into a boulder if I took my eyes off the path ahead, I held the pricey camera close to my body.

Then, suddenly, it seemed as though a giant hand pushed me toward the bottom. The monster current drove us helplessly downward and I could see the other divers reacting as I did, instinctively and futilely kicking upward. We plunged ever deeper, the sea floor ahead sloping sharply into the dark blue abyss.

Frantic, I grabbed Rigo's hand and he pulled me to his side, motioning toward a huge boulder jutting into our path some distance ahead. Instead of angling to go around it, we turned in the water to meet it feet first. I prayed the current would hold us against the rock, preventing further descent. We desperately needed time to think, to plan.

We struck the hard surface and I felt the jolt throughout my entire body, but my knees cushioned the blow. Held there by the same huge hand that had previously been shoving us downward, I watched my friends zoom past and disappear from view. Horrified, I knew I might never see them again.

Clinging to the rock, I knew we had to find a way out of the down-current. The compressed air in our tanks would cause nitrogen narcosis beyond a depth of 130 feet. Symptoms such as feelings of euphoria, impaired decision-making, and diminished motor skills could cause us to disregard the danger and make incorrect choices concerning our safety. Continuing to descend would certainly be fatal.

Rigo and I tried to slow our breathing. We didn't want to run low on air and compound our serious situation. After a short time, using hand signals, he motioned that we should swim to our left. In the distance was another rocky upthrust we could use for refuge. I suddenly understood. If we could swim *across* the current, we might be able to get out of the strongest downward flow and ascend to a safer depth.

My gauge showed eighty-five feet. I pantomimed crawling up the rock, relieved to see Rigo nod in comprehension. We hugged the rocky slope and slowly made our way fifteen feet up the boulder like a couple of oddly-attired and very awkward mountain climbers. Thankfully, the rock wasn't sharp-edged or covered with coral that would cut through our thin dive gloves and shred the knees of our Lycra wetskins. Rough and slightly porous, the surface contained nooks and niches for finger holds and the rock sloped enough that we had no trouble shimmying upward. Our fins prevented us from using our toes to gain further purchase, but the current helped hold us in place.

When the rock narrowed, we stopped and took each other's hand. Our eyes met and we nodded, simultaneously launching ourselves off, kicking hard to the left. We flew through the water and for a while I thought we were going to soar past the next big boulder, but it suddenly loomed large in front of us. We turned and met it feet-first. My gauge read ninety feet.

We rested briefly, shimmied twenty feet to the uppermost portion, and again hurled ourselves into the current. When we finally thudded into the next large rock, my gauge showed ninety-five feet. I looked at my watch to see how long we'd been in the water and found it had been the longest eighteen minutes of my life. Concerned about our depth and bottom time, I checked the laminated NAUI dive chart I wore clipped to my

BC. According to the tables, we needed to begin ascending soon or we could end up with the bends. This, too, could be fatal.

We had no choice but to keep moving. This peak was taller than the others and we crawled up to seventy feet before once more taking flight. I thought the flow seemed less powerful and hoped it wasn't just wishful thinking, but when my feet hit the next rock, the impact was much less forceful. I knew we'd reached the outer edge of the current. Almost afraid to check the time, I said a short prayer before raising my wrist.

We'd been underwater for a total of twenty-two minutes and had yet to begin our ascent. The NAUI tables indicated we must hang at fifteen feet for five minutes to offgas enough nitrogen to surface safely. *Would we have enough air?* I reached for Rigo's gauge – only 150psi. Mine read 200. We would normally finish with no less than 500psi in each tank, leaving enough air for the ascent. The good news was that as we ascended, the air would expand. But we needed to start up immediately.

We crept to the pinnacle and took off at a depth of sixty feet. I felt a distinct difference in the force of the down-current and we actually made some slight upward progress. The current lessened more and more as we drifted. No more boulders loomed in front of us and I checked my gauge to find we had ascended to fifty feet. Finally we were heading in the right direction. I pointed upward.

Turning vertical in the water, still holding hands, we worked our way toward the surface. At thirty feet, I checked the time – twenty-five total minutes. I slowed our ascent and held up my wrist. Rigo nodded to indicate he knew we'd have to decompress.

At the appointed depth, we stopped and faced each other. The water seemed choppy and we had difficulty maintaining the fifteen foot depth but it was imperative that we offgas nitrogen before surfacing. Anxious to board the boat, I'd even welcome a bout of seasickness right now. I just wanted *out* of the water.

We tried to relax and breathe normally although we'd both used up precious air fighting the current and I knew Rigo's tank would soon be empty. Time seemed to stop as I watched the second hand creep slowly around the dial. With one full minute remaining, Rigo reached for my octopus – a secondary regulator that can be used to buddy breathe. His tank was empty. Afraid to look and see how much air was in mine, I figured it was irrelevant, anyway. We'd breathe this tank down to nothing and then surface to deal with the consequences.

In short order, we sucked the last bit of air from the tank and kicked slowly upward. As we pulled the regulators out of our mouths and gulped for air, we got another shock. Directly overhead, ugly storm clouds hung low and threatening. Wind howled, waves tossed us high in the air and then dunked us in the trough, and rain poured down in sheets. Thunder boomed across the water and lightning flashed repeatedly against the black sky. And the boat was nowhere to be seen.

Shouting to be heard over the tumultuous storm, I yelled, "Where's the boat? He didn't *leave* us here, did he?" Turning in a frantic 360-degree circle, I searched in vain for the vessel. The only time I had any view at all was when the waves carried us to the crest, right before dropping us back into the trough, and all I saw in every direction was miles and miles of rough water.

Rigo cursed Captain Carlos then in his next breath offered a plausible excuse for his absence. "He could not see our bubbles een thees water. Had to save hees boat – thees storm ees un diablo." He held onto my BC and showed me where to hold his; we *had* to stay together. I wondered what had happened to my friends. *Did they survive the down-current or had it swept them to their deaths? Were they frantically searching for the boat at the surface, scared and alone, as we were?*

I suddenly had another frightening thought and yelled over the storm's noise. "Rigo, what do we do about sharks? How do we protect ourselves?" I shuddered at the idea of teeth biting into my legs from below, dragging me under.

His shouted reply surprised me but brought a small measure of comfort. "When beeg storms come, sharks go deep to be safe. There ees no danger." He looked up at the black sky and added, "Not from them."

A sudden strong wave lifted us high and when we dropped again, our tanks crashed into each other. The back of my head slammed hard against the metal valve and I hoped I wasn't bleeding. Even with Rigo's assurance that sharks dove deep during storms, I didn't want to bloody the water. Rubbing the back of my head, I said, "Rigo, let's release our tanks. They're useless now and I just hit my head on the valve." He nodded and I turned in the water. The waves heaved us to and fro and he had trouble undoing the latch securing the tank to my BC. Meanwhile, I held onto him with my left hand and used my right to release the connecting hose in front. We pushed the steel tank away from us, watching it slowly sink and disappear. Then he turned his back to me and I fought to undo his.

When both tanks had dropped out of sight, I reached for my weight belt. Then, I had another idea. I pulled myself close to Rigo and yelled into his ear. "Why don't we free our weights but use the belts to lash ourselves together? Then we won't get separated."

I couldn't believe he could flirt at a time like this, but his reply did make me smile. "You are smart, too, pretty chica. Es un buen idea."

Since we had dumped our tanks, we blew into the manual inflation tube – similar to blowing up a balloon – to inflate our BCs. We wanted to be as buoyant as possible. Then, one at a time, we removed our weights from the belts. The lead sank quickly. I buckled my belt back around my waist, but lengthened it so it was no longer snug. Rigo lengthened his and fed it through mine. In this way, after he'd refastened his belt, we were securely attached without having to physically hold onto each other.

I didn't relish spending much time being tossed about like flotsam on an angry sea, but there was nothing more we could do. Nothing except pray.

SAMPLE CHAPTER 2

Joanne

I SAW LISSY AND RIGO enter the water, followed by several others of our group. I was suited up but my dive knife had disappeared and I was loath to go without it, so four of us spent a few minutes searching. Tom gleefully announced, "Found it!" as he pulled it from under one of the bench seats. I buckled it securely to my leg.

Tom, Robbie, Sarah, and I rolled backwards off the boat. Finning toward the bottom, I saw the rest of the troupe ahead and relaxed. Captain Carlos's warning to not get separated from the group had been playing a loop in my head. We stayed close, soaring over the bottom and playing "airplane." Arms outstretched, we flew like small single-engine planes, tilting and turning to avoid the humongous rocks.

Suddenly, the current switched from fun and exhilarating to terrifyingly uncontrollable. Forced downward, I saw the bottom slope sharply away into the depths. We kicked upward to no avail, grabbing hands to stay together. The terror on their faces mirrored my own.

Up ahead, I saw Lissy and Rigo turn to meet a huge pillar feet-first and remain plastered to the rock face. I pointed and the others nodded. We spotted the next enormous boulder and aimed our flight so it was directly in our path. Turning in the water, we thudded hard against the rock, held in place by the forceful current. Hugging the rough surface, we tried to slow our breathing and control the panic.

I'd been diving for several years but had never encountered anything like this. We had to maintain control and think this through or we'd never survive. I quickly took stock of my buddies' strengths and weaknesses. Except for Sarah, we often dove together as a group so I knew them rather well.

Past middle-age, Tom was a veteran diver and very fit and strong; he was our best asset. About six feet tall, he sported broad shoulders and a severe buzz-style to his gun-metal grey hair. A widower, his great personality, quick wit, great smile, kind-heartedness, and wonderful sense of humor often hid behind his military bearing. Retired from the Navy, Tom was well-acquainted with anything to do with the sea and dove as often as possible. I had every confidence he could help save us. But we all had to do our part.

Robbie was older, a retired college professor. He was a less experienced diver but very competent and level-headed, more nerdy than athletic. Kind and compassionate, he'd had a reputation as a demanding but fair teacher and his students had always seemed to enjoy his classes. His intelligence and self-control would also be an advantage. Tall and lean, his wild head of wavy white hair gave him a "nutty professor" look but he had a big heart and I knew he loved the outdoors. He'd only discovered a passion for diving in the last year or so, but had studiously attacked the books and took the underwater exams very seriously. What he lacked in experience, he made up for in book-smarts. Another asset.

Sarah was the least experienced of our group. About thirty-five, she was a slim brunette, her long, dark hair whipping in the current like a flag in a high wind. Relatively new to the sport, she had signed up for this trip as a spontaneous gesture to her commitment to become a more proficient diver. Not at all equipped to handle this type of situation, her terror showed plainly in her huge eyes. Bubbles billowed from her regulator. She had to calm down and breathe slower or she'd run out of air far too quickly. I vowed to do my best to help her through this.

Sarah crushed my hand in a vise-like grip. I turned my head to meet her eyes and pointed to her regulator, then fluttered my fingers quickly upward, mimicking her bubbles. Letting the current hold me against the rock, I forced my fingers out of her grasp. I patted my chest to indicate breathing, and then put my arms at my sides, hands waist high. I slowly pushed my palms toward the sea floor, much as I'd seen my yoga instructor do when she wanted us to exhale slowly. I pointed to Sarah to do the same. She nodded. We repeated this movement several times until her eyes lost that crazed, panicky look and the amount of bubbles flowing from her regulator lessened.

I made a circle with the thumb and first finger of my right hand, the universal scuba sign meaning "Are you okay?" She nodded and repeated the okay signal back to me. I turned to Tom and motioned that we should swim to the next big rock.

But instead of pushing off, he gestured upward and began crawling up the rock face. When the peak became too narrow for four of us abreast he stopped and pointed toward the next boulder. I understood that he wanted us to lose some depth before diving back into the current.

Still holding hands, we launched off the pinnacle, kicking as hard as we could to the left. In a short time, we landed on the next rock, working our way *across* the current to escape the worst of the down-flow.

When I saw Tom check his watch and examine his NAUI tables, I knew we might also have another problem. We had to keep moving to try and reach the surface as soon as possible, minimizing our bottom time. He looked up and met my gaze. I could see the worry in his eyes.

We repeated the climb-and-flight-to-the-next-rock routine several times and finally the current lessened. I hoped we'd soon find Lissy and Rigo waiting on the boat. This was one dive I was anxious to end.

As we clung to the last pillar before ascending, Tom showed us his NAUI tables. He pointed out the box that showed we needed to hang at fifteen feet for five minutes to offgas nitrogen before surfacing. We all reached for our gauges: 150psi; 120psi; 100psi; and 60psi. Sarah had, indeed, used up a lot of air in her initial panic.

We hurled ourselves into the much-diminished current and Tom led us upward at a safe rate. As we ascended, I could sense Sarah's building terror – now out of the monster current she was frantic to reach the surface. I held her hand tightly, afraid she'd bolt. Rising faster than her exhaled air bubbles could cause the bends and I wanted to protect her.

At the prescribed fifteen feet, Tom stopped. I gripped both of Sarah's hands and turned to face her. I could see the raw panic in her eyes. She looked upward and yanked one hand free, kicking desperately for the surface. Tom and Robbie both grabbed for her BC. Her flailing fist knocked my mask off and I instinctively let go of her to replace it and clear the water from around my nose. Her other fist hit Tom on the temple and momentarily dazed him. Robbie held Sarah's BC with one hand as he checked her remaining air. At that moment, bubbles stopped flowing from her regulator and her eyes grew even wider – her tank was empty. As I reached toward her with my octopus, she jerked free of Robbie's one-handed grip and bolted for the surface.

I started after her, but Tom grabbed me and vehemently shook his head no. We still had three minutes remaining to offgas and there was nothing we could do for Sarah now that she was at the surface. Nitrogen bubbles in her blood would have expanded and lodged in her system. And, inexperienced diver that she was, she had most likely held her breath during the race to the surface possibly also causing an air embolism.

Looking upward, I could see her lying face down at the surface, eyes open, immobile and tossed by the waves. She was only fifteen feet away and I couldn't help. A nurse by profession, it went against my very being to do nothing, but helping her would put myself at grave risk, too. Tears burned my eyes. *What had happened to the rest of our group? Had the sea claimed more than one life today?*

Robbie pulled his regulator from his mouth to show he was out of air. We checked our gauges and I handed my octopus to Robbie to buddy breathe. Soon, all the tanks would be empty.

The three of us faced each other, held hands, and tried to slow our breathing. It became harder and harder to suck a breath from my tank. Tom was watching, ready with his octopus when we drained the last of the air. He handed it to me for a breath, I handed it to Robbie who then handed it back to Tom. In this way, we finished off the final tank. With no other option remaining, we slowly finned to the surface, exhaling as we went. I hoped we'd off-gassed enough nitrogen to avoid the bends.

The world as we knew it when we'd entered the water earlier no longer existed. Thunder boomed, lightning flashed against the angry purple-black sky, and rain poured down in buckets. Waves carried us high and then dunked us back under water, leaving us spluttering and coughing. Sarah's body had drifted away, buffeted by the storm and the howling wind. We didn't even have a chance to say good-bye.

Terror claimed us once more. The boat was gone and we were alone on a storm-tossed sea. Again, retired Navy man Tom came to our rescue. We released our empty tanks, manually inflated our BCs, and removed the lead from our weight belts. Lashing ourselves together with the nylon belts, we took a small measure of comfort in the physical closeness. There was nothing more we could do. I closed my eyes and spoke to God. I hoped He was listening.

STRANDED is Book #2 of the Savage Creation Series and is available in ebook and paperback formats so you can find out how Lissy and her friends survive the storm and the angry sea — and all the dangers they face on a beautiful yet perilous deserted island.

Book #1 in the Savage Creations Series is Savage Isle.

CONNECT WITH BEVERLEY SCHERBERGER

BEVERLEY WELCOMES emails and comments.

You can contact me on my Facebook page – I respond to all comments.

And I'd love a review on Amazon, if you'd take just one more minute.

Thanks!

Bev

http://www.facebook.com/beverley.scherberger

Made in the USA
Columbia, SC
01 March 2022

57035671R00071